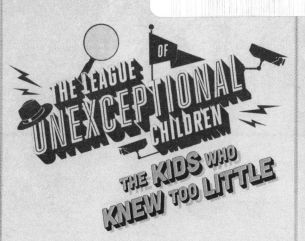

THE LEAGUE OF UNEXCEPTIONAL CHILDREN

THE KIDS WHO KNEW TOO LITTLE

BY GITTY DANESHVARI

ILLUSTRATED BY JAMES LANCETT

LITTLE, BROWN BOOKS FOR YOUNG READERS
www.lbkids.co.uk

LITTLE, BROWN BOOKS FOR YOUNG READERS

First published in the US in 2017 by Little, Brown and Company
First published in Great Britain in 2017 by Hodder and Stoughton

1 3 5 7 9 10 8 6 4 2

A CIP catalogue record for this book
is available from the British Library.

ISBN 978-0-349-12422-3

Printed and bound by CPI Group (UK) Ltd, Croydon, CR0 4YY

The paper and board used in this book are
made from wood from responsible sources.

MIX
Paper from
responsible sources
FSC® C104740

Little, Brown Books for Young Readers
An imprint of
Hachette Children's Group
Part of Hodder and Stoughton
Carmelite House
50 Victoria Embankment
London EC4Y 0DZ

An Hachette UK Company
www.hachette.co.uk

www.hachettechildrens.co.uk

For Priscilla Alden Sailer

"Thomas Edison once said genius is 1% inspiration and 99% perspiration, which means smart people must *really* smell."

—Candela Gabriel, 13, Bar Harbor, Maine

CHAPTER 1

<098762-CG-LOUC-101>

NOVEMBER 2, 1:16 A.M. TUNNEL. BULGARIA
Darkness rolled in like clouds of an impending
storm. Two figures, small in stature, trudged slowly
along. A stench, thick and rancid, burned their nostrils, dripping down their throats and souring their
stomachs. Sludge trickled off the cement walls of the
tunnel, meandered through their hair, and stained
their already filthy clothes. Nearly a hundred feet
belowground, the temperature soared and the air
thinned. *Keep going*, they told themselves, *just keep
going*. Freedom would soon be found. They had

come so far; it couldn't end here. Could it? *No!* they screamed to themselves. *No! We will fight until the end! We are members of the League of Unexceptional Children! We were chosen for a reason!*

Oh yes, but that reason...that reason was hardly comforting. They were chosen for their *lack* of intelligence, athletic prowess, and memorability. They were chosen because they were nobodies, kids so inconsequential, they were often mistaken for furniture.

"*Occulta potentia in umbra. Occulta potentia in umbra. Occulta potentia in umbra. Occulta potentia in umbra...*" voices chanted in the distance.

And yet, somehow, the nobodies had become the hunted.

Racing through the tunnel, muck splashing against their legs, twelve-year-old Jonathan Murray and Shelley Brown felt capture closing in on them. There was no more luck to be mined. There were no more exceptions for the unexceptionals. The end was near; they could feel it.

Louder and louder the voices grew: "*Occulta potentia in umbra. Occulta potentia in umbra. Occulta potentia in umbra...*"

A meaningless assortment of sounds, that's what these words were to Jonathan and Shelley. After all, the two had a hard enough time with English, let alone Latin. And yet the words ignited a terror so deep in them that they could hardly breathe. *This shall be the soundtrack of our deaths*, they thought.

"*Occulta potentia in umbra...*"

Chests tightened. Heavy. Painful. As though dipped in quick-drying cement, their lungs struggled for each breath. *Keep going*, they told themselves, death's shadow seemingly closer by the second. Were these to be their last moments on earth? Alone, plodding through a murky tunnel, hope fading rapidly?

"I can't..." Jonathan muttered, saliva pooling beneath his tongue, sickness rising in his throat.

Crashing slowly to his knees, Jonathan retched the last contents of his stomach. Not since an unfortunate incident with tapioca pudding (full disclosure: Mrs. Murray considers expiration dates little more than numerical decorations) had he experienced such a violent revolt from within his body. Flickers of light dotted his vision and muddled his mind. Much like a cartoon, Jonathan's eyes rolled so far back in his head, the irises were no longer visible.

"Oh no," Shelley said as she began to dry heave, her words drowned out by guttural noises. "Argh... no... argh... argh... stop, please stop, you're making me sick."

"I think I'm dying," Jonathan mumbled as Shelley's gagging trailed off.

"In the sense that we're all dying someday?"

Jonathan shook his head as Shelley attempted to lift him to his feet. "I can't go on. I'm too weak."

"*Occulta potentia in umbra. Occulta potentia in umbra...*"

"Stop pretending, Johno—get up!" Shelley insisted, tears falling from beneath her filthy glasses.

"I'll try and stop them as best I can, even if only for a minute," Jonathan whispered. "Just keep going."

"I'm not leaving you here to die," Shelley said, her mind blurring with memories of the two of them—climbing through the fridge at League headquarters, saving the vice president, traipsing through London, risking everything to stop the release of a virus capable of dimming one's intelligence, laughter, khaki slacks,

Hammett Humphries, Nurse Maidenkirk. "Shells and Johno go together like pickles and ranch dressing, like Coca-Cola and milk—"

"Those sound disgusting. . . ."

"Exactly! You'd never think they would go together, but they do. Kind of like us," Shelley said. "So I'm not leaving here without you even if that means I have to carry you."

"I'll only slow you down."

It was true. Jonathan was to be the brick that cemented their demise. And yet Shelley persevered, wrapping his limp arm around her neck.

"We're getting out of here one way or another. Nothing can stop us. Not even death! Or actually, on second thought, death could totally stop us, which is why we need to start praying we get caught!" Shelley whispered excitedly.

"What?" Jonathan responded as they staggered down the tunnel, the chant continuing in the background like a song stuck on repeat.

"*Occulta potentia in umbra. Occulta potentia in umbra . . .*"

"God has never answered any of my prayers. Not a one. Grow an extra inch over the summer?

5

Denied! Have a face that people remember? Denied! Win a talent show and become famous enough to have my own reality show? Denied! Read animals' minds? Denied! Be the first kid in the world to add God as a friend on Facebook? Denied!"

"You think God's on Facebook?"

"He…or she…even denied small requests like having a cheese-and-avocado sandwich dropped off at my house."

"God is not a delivery service, Shells."

"That is not the point!"

"*Occulta potentia in umbra. Occulta potentia in umbra. Occulta potentia in umbra…*"

"Shells, you're not making any sense!"

"I'm praying for them to catch us, because then it won't happen!"

Jonathan raised his eyebrows incredulously. "You're trying to use reverse psychology on God?"

"What choice do I have? It's either that or rely on *Charl*!"

Jonathan and Shelley both shook their heads and sighed—a long and heavy sigh. The kind reserved for such annoyances as school talent shows, lines at an amusement park, and teachers who give homework on Fridays.

"The *h* is silent, remember?"

Jonathan and Shelley jumped as a boy's voice emerged from the darkness.

"Did I just hear *Ch*arl remind us *yet again* that his name is pronounced 'Carl'?!" Shelley barked as a boy, whose skin was covered head to toe in freckles and moles, creating a natural camouflage effect, stepped toward them. The boy could *literally* fade into the background, whether it be a bush, wallpaper, or in this case a sludge-coated tunnel.

"Crazy running into you guys like this, right?" Carl said with the casualness one might expect in a supermarket or even the dentist's office, but not an underground tunnel in Bulgaria.

"Why are you here? You told us you were going to get help! Call for reinforcements!" Jonathan growled, his anger palpable.

"Yeah, about that...looks like it's not going to happen...."

"Gee, you think?" Shelley scoffed.

"I tried....Actually, I didn't try, I just followed

7

you guys. So no one's coming—well, except for the maniacs. They're definitely coming."

"*Occulta potentia in umbra. Occulta potentia in umbra. Occulta potentia in umbra. Occulta potentia in umbra.*"

"Charl, I hate you. I really do."

"You're trying to use reverse psychology on me, aren't you?" Carl said with a sly smile. "Good news: It's working. I love you, Selley."

"It's Shelley!"

"You sure the *h* isn't silent? It's more common than you think. Carl, Fred, Jerry, Alex—"

"None of those names have *h*'s in them," Jonathan pointed out.

"Or maybe the *h*'s are just invisible?"

"*Occulta potentia in umbra. Occulta potentia in umbra…*"

"We don't have time for this!" Jonathan snapped.

Shelley raised her hand to stop the others from talking. "Do you hear that?"

"The sound of impending doom is kind of hard to miss," Jonathan answered.

"On that note, I think it's time for me to blend

into the background," Carl said, before adding, "But if you need me to relay a message or return a library book or something, just let me know."

Shelley balled her hands into fists and growled. "Stop talking and listen!"

Thhhhh. Thluck. Thhhhh. Thluck.

"Water's trickling down! That means there's a drain nearby—a possible way out!" Shelley explained as she dropped to her knees and frantically felt around the tunnel floor. Fleshy, phlegm-like lumps of mud passed through her fingers as she searched for the cool touch of metal. "I found it, but it's too heavy. I need your help, Charl!"

"But I'm blending into the background to avoid being killed so that I can live...and return your library books.... What about Jonathan?"

"Khaki's almost dead! He can't lift anything! Come on, Charl, do something right for once!" Shelley said.

Almost dead? Jonathan thought. It was true that he couldn't remember a time when he had felt so depleted, so tired, so utterly devoid of hope. He imagined his skin gray and chalky, his eyes dulled,

9

and his lips cracked with spots of blood breaking through. Maybe he *was* about to die.

"Ugh," Shelley grunted as she and Carl attempted to lift the drain.

Jonathan's stomach sank. This was it. This was the moment their unexceptionalness—specifically their lack of physical strength—was going to get them all killed.

"*Occulta potentia in umbra. Occulta potentia in umbra…*"

"Guys, there's no way we're lifting this drain," Carl said nonchalantly as the chanting grew closer. "Which means this is the end of the road for you two, aka time to pick out coffins. Speaking of which, my uncle can get you a good deal. They don't call him the King of Coffins for nothing."

"*Occulta potentia in umbra. Occulta potentia in umbra.*"

"I'm not ready to die! Or maybe I'm already dead? Is this…Did I fail heaven's entrance exam? I knew I shouldn't have cut the head off my sister's doll!" Shelley rambled hysterically, tears dribbling down her cheeks.

Jonathan looked Shelley in the eye and noted

10

the disappearance of her irrational optimism, that annoying quality that had always left him with a mixture of envy and irritation. The stress of the situation had gnawed at her, and now she was unraveling right before Jonathan's eyes. So he mustered every last ounce of energy he had and presented a self-assured, confident facade. "That doll deserved to have her head cut off.... Wait, that didn't come out right."

"It did if you're trying to sound like one of those crazy people who push strangers in front of trains," Carl explained. "Which is one of my fears: death by train. I'm also afraid of death by hot dog cart, death by cat scratch fever, death by crazed maniacs in a tunnel...."

Jonathan shot Carl a look, took a deep breath, and started again. "What I meant to say was heaven would be lucky to have you, Shells. But unless you're in a rush to get there, we need to start jumping."

"Jumping?" Shelley repeated.

Jonathan nodded. "If we can't lift the grate, maybe we can break through it?"

"Talk about a khaki-coated genius," Shelley said as the two began jumping up and down.

"*Occulta potentia in umbra. Occulta potentia in umbra…*"

"I've never been one for long good-byes," Carl said as he stepped toward Jonathan and Shelley and threw his arms around them. "Keep in touch…if they don't kill you, that is."

Creeeeaaaakkk. Creeeaaakkk.

"No!" Carl screamed as the grate dropped out from beneath them.

"Shhhhh!!!" Jonathan and Shelley responded as they free-fell through the unknown. Swathed

in darkness, all they could do was hope that what awaited them was safer than what was chasing them.

Thud!

NOVEMBER 2, 3:17 A.M. ORDER OF MERIUM. BULGARIA

What happened? Jonathan thought as he slowly roused to consciousness. *My head hurts. No, wait—everything hurts*, the boy noted as he opened his eyes. So dark was the room, he wondered if he might be blindfolded. Unable to move, his arms and legs tied tightly, he called out for his friend.

"Shells?"

"Johno?" Shelley offered faintly, "I can't move."

"Neither can I," Jonathan answered.

"Guys," Carl chimed in, "I'm here too, just in case you want to check on me."

Jonathan and Shelley shook their heads. Carl was beginning to feel like a shadow, always creeping around behind them. But before they could even finish their thoughts, they heard *it*.

"*Occulta potentia in umbra. Occulta potentia in umbra…*"

"No!" Jonathan and Shelley shrieked as the lights switched on.

Their voices grew hoarse, their veins throbbed visibly across their necks, and their limbs trembled. Seated back to back in chairs, Jonathan, Shelley, and Carl took in the figures surrounding them, cloaked in black velvet floor-length robes and red masks. Deformed and drooping, the masks' features appeared melted, much like a crayon left in the afternoon sun.

"White," Carl mumbled in dismay as he looked at the stark floor and walls. "It's my kryptonite. I can't blend with white!"

"Gentlemen…and maybe ladies…it's hard to tell with these outfits," Shelley said as her grubby glasses slid down the bridge of her nose. "I know what you're thinking: Let's just kill these kids and call it a day. Maybe sing that terrible song a few more times and go to bed?"

"Shells? What are you doing?" Jonathan whispered.

"Shelltastic doesn't give up without a fight or a speech," Shelley answered before turning her attention back to the masked figures. "But here's the

14

thing: We're as strong as steel. As loyal as a blind dog. And as devilish as a ... deviled egg at a cocktail party ... one that has gone bad ... as in you're going to have food poisoning for at least two days."

A figure carrying a candelabra stepped forward and slowly lowered the ornate silver antique over Shelley, hot wax dribbling across the back of her hand.

"Ahhhh! Stop it! That hurts!"

"So," Jonathan said, too numb to shout or cry or do any of the other things he would have expected, "*this* is the end."

A scratchy voice replied, "No, *this* is only the beginning...."

"How come my mom
uses air quotes whenever
she calls me smart?"

—Everett Berry, 10, Madison, Mississippi

CHAPTER 2

<098762-JA-LOUC-101>

THREE DAYS EARLIER

OCTOBER 30, 1:02 P.M. PLANE. SOMEWHERE
OVER THE ATLANTIC

"Ugh," Jonathan grumbled while seated next to
Shelley at the back of a crowded plane. "I don't feel
so good."

"Johno, I'm no doctor, although I'm pretty sure
I could pass for one if there was no blood involved.
Like, I could be a really good fake dermatologist."

"Uhhhh," Jonathan interrupted, covering his mouth as he burped.

"Anyway, as I was saying, I'm no doctor, but I'm pretty sure you're in the throes of a junk-food hangover. By my count, you've ingested forty-two packets of peanuts, ten bags of potato chips, thirteen Coca-Colas, and three candy bars so far on the flight."

Jonathan looked down at the floor surrounding his cramped airplane seat, littered with junk-food wrappers and crumpled soda cans, and nodded. "I don't even remember eating half this stuff."

"I do," Shelley said. "You tend to chew very loudly when you're stressed. It was like sitting next to a chipmunk for the last six hours...*chmmm*... *chmmm*...."

Ignoring Shelley, Jonathan shook his head. "I still can't believe it. Hammett says my parents stole classified government documents. They committed treason? How is that possible? They don't even know who the president is. They think the House and the Senate are names of bands. They ask me on a regular basis if taxes are optional. They still don't know the difference between *their*, *there*, and *they're*!

My mother performed a cheer at my grandfather's funeral and she didn't understand why people were offended. *'You're dead, you're dead, Mother said you're dead. We're sad, we're sad, we're going to miss you, Dad!'* " Jonathan remembered.

"Cheerleading at a funeral?" Shelley remarked. "I'm kind of impressed."

"There must be some sort of explanation. Maybe it's a case of mistaken identity," Jonathan muttered, both of his hands atop his head.

"Johno, it's time to face the facts," Shelley said as she placed her hand on the boy's shoulder. "Your mom and dad, aka Carmen and Mickey Murray, are currently sitting in the clink. And it's not because they forgot to mow their lawn for the last twelve years or because they fed the animals at the zoo, even though the sign explicitly says not to.... Your parents are being held at the CIA, which means they've done something *really bad*."

"You don't understand; your parents are geniuses. If they were caught spying, we would know they knew what they were doing. But *my* parents? They must have been manipulated or tricked. They're intellectually challenged. Oh, forget it, who am I kidding? They're dumb! Anyone could trick them!"

Shelley nodded. "And just to clarify, the *they're* you just mentioned, it's spelled *t-h-e-y*-apostrophe-*r-e*, right?"

Jonathan's eyes widened. "Are you even listening to me? My parents have been arrested for the worst crime imaginable!"

"I think you'll find that if you ask Nurse Maidenkirk, there are a lot worse crimes out there, but I get what you're saying....It's bad...really bad... especially since *you're a spy and all....*" Shelley trailed off.

"What do you mean?"

"Hammett and President Arons might wonder if you're working with your parents."

Jonathan pointed to himself. "Me? I can barely handle being a spy, let alone a double agent! How smart do they think I am?"

"Actually, they don't think you're smart at all— that's why they recruited you for the League."

Jonathan gave Shelley a steely look.

"That was a rhetorical question, wasn't it?" Shelley said, furrowing her brow. "I just don't get it—why ask a question if you don't want to hear the answer? It's like ordering a meal you aren't going to eat!"

"There has to be some other explanation. There just has to be. I know my parents. They're not spies."

"They would probably say the exact same thing about you. But having met your parents, my gut tells me you're right. And my gut is never wrong, except about dairy products and a few other things. Bottom line, my gut is *mostly* right. Like fifty-eight percent of the time, which now that I think about it is an F," Shelley babbled as Jonathan looked ahead, lost in thought.

"More peanuts?" a stewardess asked, pushing a cart down the aisle.

"Come on, lady. What are you doing? Trying to kill him?" Shelley scoffed before pulling out a newspaper from the seat pocket in front of her and then shaking her head. "This is seriously messed up."

"Let me guess," Jonathan droned, his stomach turning with anticipation. "My parents were behind the Kennedy assassination?"

"Who's Kennedy?"

Jonathan narrowed his eyes. "Really, Shells? You don't know who John F. Kennedy was?"

21

"Oh, him? Of course I do. He's the guy they named the airport after in New York."

"I don't even know how to respond."

"Then don't," Shelley said as she held up the paper, featuring a large photo of Carmen and Mickey Murray. "Your parents are officially famous, which means *you're famous*, which is totally unfair because I have always wanted to be famous! Remember the Change.org petition I started, *Make Shelley Brown Famous or She'll Cut Off a Toe*?!"

"The Internet is a weird place," Jonathan said, shaking his head. "Or maybe you're just weird."

"Why did I have to get stuck with scientists for parents? Who cares about curing cancer? I would make an awesome daughter of internationally known criminals!"

"Do you even hear yourself?"

Shelley nodded. "I do, and honestly, half the time I can't even believe what I'm saying."

OCTOBER 30, 3:43 P.M. TAXI. WASHINGTON, DC

Seated next to Jonathan in the back of a nondescript yellow cab, Shelley looked absolutely crest-

22

fallen. She was a shell of her usual animated self, everything from her eyebrows to her lips drooping toward the floor in a sign of total emotional annihilation.

"*The Son of Spies*," Shelley blurted out in a cold, monotone manner.

"Excuse me?"

"That's the title of your memoir," Shelley said, before adding, "Oh, and you're welcome. With that title, it's sure to be a bestseller."

"Shells? My parents are facing life in prison, possibly even death! And you're jealous?! That's deranged!" Jonathan snapped as the taxi entered the always-immaculate town of Evanston, Virginia. Though in the throes of a major scandal—"Local Dog Walkers Arrested for Espionage," read the morning paper—the town looked as pristine as ever with uniformly cut lawns and freshly polished cars.

"Is that a clinical diagnosis? Derangement? Because right now, I could really use something to make me feel special, even if it is a mental disorder."

"That comment alone should ensure safe passage to the sanitarium of your choice," Jonathan said before dropping his head into his hands.

Ever since Jonathan first heard the news, he had fought diligently to keep one very frightening thought at bay. Was it possible his parents weren't who he thought they were? Could they actually be spies? Had they been pretending to be dumb all these years? Was he the sole idiot in the family? Jonathan had always taken a certain amount of solace in the fact that his parents were challenged in the intelligence department. With genetics like that, he didn't dare hope for anything more than average. But if they were in fact spies, then they must be brilliant too. For no one short of a genius could pull off this level of deception. And that was simply too much to bear: to be the only butter knife in a family of machetes.

"I think my head's going to explode," Jonathan said as he winced, sharp pain flashing like lightning behind his eyes.

Yet another claim to fame: the boy whose head exploded, Shelley thought as the taxi came to a stop.

"You kids sure this is the right address?" the driver called out as he parked in front of the Murray residence, which was swarming with news vans, reporters, looky-loos, and nosy neighbors.

"This is the right address," Jonathan droned as he handed the driver cash, grabbed his suitcase, and pushed open the door.

Walking a few steps behind Jonathan, Shelley carefully took in the back of her friend—plain white shirt, khaki slacks, hunched shoulders that said "Don't bother looking at me; I'm no one." This was it—these were to be Jonathan's last moments of anonymity. From here on out, he would be Jonathan Murray, son of spies—forcing Shelley to once again retreat to a world where Zelda the goldfish took top honors as her best friend.

"Johno! Wait!" Shelley said seconds before the boy reached the back of the crowd. "Could you do me a favor?"

"Now?"

"It will only take a second."

"Fine," Jonathan acquiesced, motioning for Shelley to hurry.

"Would you mind telling the reporters that your parents have been holding me hostage the last few years? Using me as an indentured servant, kind of like Cinderella. Maybe even drop the name Shellerella?"

Jonathan shook his head, turned, and walked straight into the throng of people.

"Is that a yes?" Shelley called out, trailing a few feet behind the boy.

"Excuse me! Let me through! I live here!" Jonathan screamed as he tried to penetrate the wall of bodies surrounding his house.

"Get out of here!" a reporter snarled as he stepped in front of Jonathan, blocking his path.

Red in the face, stressed, sweating, and dragging a suitcase, Jonathan exploded.

"NO! I will not get out of here! I LIVE HERE!

My name is Jonathan Murray and I am Carmen and Mickey's son! Now move it!" Jonathan announced in a voice so loud and authoritative that it shocked Shelley and momentarily quelled the boisterous crowd.

So this was the new Jonathan, Shelley thought as she experienced a mixture of both awe and jealousy. Was it possible that her friend with the flat black hair, poor posture, and painfully boring clothes was now a cool, tough-talking dude?

"It's not that you're a loser, you just *seem* like a loser. There's a difference."

—Joe Atfield, 14, New Canaan, Connecticut, speaking to himself in the mirror

CHAPTER 3

<098762-JA-LOUC-101>

OCTOBER 30, 4:20 P.M. THE MURRAY RESIDENCE. EVANSTON, VIRGINIA

"The Murrays don't have any children," a neighbor yelled from the crowd.

"Yeah," another seconded. "I've lived next door to the Murrays for fifteen years and I've never so much as seen this kid!"

"Mr. Donaldson? I spent three days in your basement after your son forgot he was playing hide-and-seek with me!"

Hide-and-seek was a dangerous game for unexceptionals. Why, the League was littered with stories of children who passed days, sometimes even a week under beds, in closets, or behind curtains—all the while desperately waiting to be found.

"What are you trying to do? Get the scoop for the school paper?" a reporter asked Jonathan as he pulled him by the collar of his shirt and dropped him on the curb. "This is a matter for professionals."

"But I'm telling the truth! I live here! Carmen and Mickey are my parents!"

"There are about thirty-five of the best reporters in the country here today. Trust me, if these two traitors had a son, we'd know about it."

From behind, a familiar gravelly voice interrupted. "Look here, kid, this is no place for a pipsqueak like you. So why don't you take this fiver and go get yourself a hot dog."

Upon hearing the man's voice, Jonathan looked up and smiled.

Hammett Humphries. Tall. Hair slicked back. Dressed in a double-breasted gray pinstripe suit. Toothpick dangling from the corner of his mouth. Lurking

30

behind him, dressed in her usual white uniform, was the always somber-looking Nurse Maidenkirk.

"Ethel and Julius Rosenberg were executed for treason in 1953."

"Can it, Maidenkirk!" Hammett snapped before turning to Jonathan. "Like I said, why don't you go grab yourself a hot dog."

And with that, Hammett and Nurse Maidenkirk turned and walked away. Jonathan watched them cross the street, comforted by their presence. It was going to be okay; somehow, someway, it would be okay, Jonathan thought.

"It happens more than you'd think," Shelley said, approaching Jonathan. "Plants and people fighting, but as the saying goes, *It's easy to get peeved...when dealing with leaves...and thieves...and people who wear shirts without sleeves...* or something like that."

Across the street, face flushed, arms waving, Hammett was speaking animatedly to a medium-sized bush.

"Hammett's screaming at a plant?" Jonathan questioned.

"Sure looks that way," Shelley replied.

And just like that, Jonathan's hope faded.

"Hello, young lady," Shelley called out to the teenage girl standing behind the register snapping her gum and checking her phone.

"Young lady?" Jonathan repeated. "She's at least three years older than us."

"And by *young*, I am, of course, referring to the fact that I am an old soul, wise beyond my years… and behind my ears too… get it? That's where my brain is.…"

The teenage girl, totally unaware of Shelley's presence, grabbed a near-empty soda and began noisily sucking the last remnants through the straw.

"Hey!" Shelley said impatiently, tapping the girl's arm. "I'm talking to you!"

"Slow your roll, angry bird," the teenager drawled.

"Angry bird? I am neither angry nor a bird. Although if I come back in another life, I am definitely open to being a bird."

"So you can fly?"

"So I can relieve myself on the heads of irritating people like yourself!" Shelley huffed as she adjusted her glasses.

"That's one messed-up fantasy," the girl responded as Jonathan stepped forward.

"Give us a double dog with a side of mustard, two sides of relish, a diet Fanta, fourteen packets of ketchup, two straws, and seven napkins."

"Right this way," the girl said as she motioned for Jonathan and Shelley to step into the kitchen, whereby she quickly opened the fridge and removed tray after tray of hot dogs.

"Rest in peace, piggies," Shelley said. "Or should I say rest in pieces? Since you've been ground up into a million different pieces and then molded into the shape of bloated noodles."

"Well, if it isn't my favorite part-time vegetarian," Jonathan mumbled as he crawled into the cold, salty-smelling fridge, Shelley directly behind him.

Leaning down, the teenage girl smiled at Shelley and said, "Some cultures consider a bird pooping on you to be a sign of good luck."

"Then you're going to be one lucky girl in about seventy or eighty years when I come back as a bird. Although seeing as you're older than I am, you'll probably already be dead by the time I die, which means this plan, like so many before it, isn't going to work out...." Shelley trailed off as the door closed.

After two forceful thumps, the back wall of the fridge opened, dropping Jonathan and Shelley into the League's waiting room. It was exactly as they remembered—unruly orange carpet, a few chairs, a wooden desk, a black typewriter, and an elderly secretary with a beehive hairdo.

"Take a seat, children," the woman said while carefully filing her nails. "Mr. Humphries will be right out."

Hammett led Jonathan and Shelley through the
main room awash in secretaries clacking away furi-
ously on typewriters, past the throng of gray filing
cabinets, around a couple of ferns, and down a long
hall.

"Hammett?" a boy's voice called out from the
patch of greenery.

"Not now, Carl!"

Jonathan and Shelley turned toward the ferns
just as a boy, covered in moles and freckles, emerged
from the foliage. Dressed in camouflage army
fatigues, he was a natural chameleon, blending into
the background almost anywhere he went.

The voice, chipper and squeaky, asked Hammett, "Did you think about what I said?"

"Stop following me, Carl! I already told you,
you're a green banana—you're just not ready."

"Oh," Jonathan muttered to himself, "Hammett was talking to Carl...not the bush....What a
relief!"

Smiling, Carl motioned toward Jonathan and

Shelley. "Aren't you going to introduce me to your friends?"

"They're not my friends; they're my operatives," Hammett barked. "Jonathan? Shelley? Meet Carl, with a silent *h*."

"My mom slipped it in just to mess with me," Carl explained.

"So your name is Charl?" Shelley asked.

"It's pronounced 'Carl.' "

"But it's spelled *C-h-a-r-l*?" Shelley pressed on.

"Since it's a silent *h*, it's invisible."

"If it's invisible, how do you know it's there?" Shelley continued, eyeing the boy carefully.

"Oh, it's there. I can feel it," Carl assured Shelley. "It's like a piece of popcorn stuck in my throat, irritating me, making it impossible to concentrate on the movie."

Shelley nodded. She had no idea what this kid was talking about, but she could relate to the annoyance of having a piece of popcorn stuck in your throat. Try as she might, she could never ignore the feeling. She would start off with a cough that quickly turned into something akin to a cat dislodging a fur ball. All in all, it was a most unpleasant experience, which may explain, Shelley thought, why her grandmother never let her buy popcorn at the movies.

Jonathan watched Shelley watch Carl. What was she doing? Why was she still staring at him? Seconds passed. Jonathan's palms, a sweaty mess, began to tremble. Every second he stood here was another second his parents sat locked away at the CIA.

"Shells? Just a quick reminder: My parents are facing life in prison and possibly even worse, so if we could move this along I would really appreciate it," Jonathan said, the words friendly, the tone anything but.

"Sorry about that, Khaki; the popcorn comment really got to me," Shelley offered dramatically, prompting Jonathan to roll his eyes as Hammett opened the door to his office.

"This way, shorties."

"Don't worry about the hallway. I'll keep an eye on things out here," Carl hollered as Hammett closed the door.

Nurse Maidenkirk, seated in the corner of the room, nodded hello to Jonathan and Shelley while flipping through one of her favorite publications—*Taxidermy Monthly*. Pictures of deceased animals stuffed to look as though still alive put Nurse Maidenkirk at ease. It was an unusual reaction, but then again, Nurse Maidenkirk was an unusual woman. Some might even say she was a *very* unusual woman.

"Hey, Maidenkirk," Jonathan grumbled as he felt the tension mount within him. His jaw tightened, his eyes twitched, and his stomach clenched as he pondered how he had come to find himself in such a situation. How was it possible that his parents—the human equivalent of the Scarecrow from *The Wizard of Oz*—were facing charges of treason?

"Hammett," Jonathan said, his voice cracking. "Is it true? Are my parents spies?"

"I'm going to give it to you straight, kid," Hammett said as he pulled the toothpick from his mouth. "I just don't know. I've met your parents, and to be frank, they don't seem smart enough to steal ketchup from McDonald's, never mind classified documents from the US government."

Jonathan's eyes grew glassy as he fought the urge to cry. "Mom and Dad love ketchup. They keep a bottle hidden under their bed just in case aliens come by unannounced."

"I think I speak for the whole room when I say,

what?" Shelley said as she looked over her glasses at Jonathan.

"Apparently aliens love ketchup...or at least that's what my parents think," Jonathan explained.

"Here's the bottom line, kid: The evidence points to your parents using their job as dog walkers to get into the Harrington residence and download a file from their computer."

"What was the file?" Jonathan asked.

"The STS," Hammett answered.

Jonathan shook his head. "I don't know what that is."

"The Secret Tunnel System is a grid of underground passages linking the White House, the Capitol, and the Supreme Court in case of a nuclear attack. However, if the map of the tunnels were to fall into the wrong hands, it could also prove the perfect means to gain access to our country's most important buildings."

"And my parents stole the map of the STS?"

Hammett nodded.

"You have actual proof?"

"Your parents couldn't figure out how to transfer the file, so they e-mailed it to themselves. And as if that wasn't bad enough, they left their e-mail account open on the Harringtons' computer," Hammett explained, nervously fidgeting with a button on his jacket.

"Is it just me or does that seem like a big mistake for spies to make?" Shelley asked.

"It's one of the many questions we have regarding this case. There's a lot we don't understand. But we also can't overlook the evidence. And the evidence doesn't look good. To be honest, it looks bad—real bad."

"Life in prison is not a pretty thing, especially for spies. They're usually kept in solitary confinement. Most of them go crazy. But they're the lucky ones. Remember what happened to the Rosenbergs?" Nurse Maidenkirk muttered, still paging through pictures of taxidermy animals.

Shelley pursed her lips and grumbled, "Stop bringing up the Rosenbergs or I'll lock you in the closet and throw away the key...and yes, I realize there isn't a closet in here...nor do I have any keys...not even to my own house...because my grandparents don't trust me...but that's not the point...just stop talking about the Rosenbergs!"

"I need to see my mom and dad," Jonathan announced to the room, his face awash in perspiration. "Even if it's true, even if they are spies, they're still my parents."

"As far as you know," Shelley supposed. "After all, they betrayed their country. Who's to say they didn't kidnap you? Maybe your real name is Arnold and you're from one big khaki-wearing family?"

"Arnold?" Nurse Maidenkirk repeated. "I could see that."

"So now they're spies *and* kidnappers?" Jonathan exclaimed as he shook his head.

"Cool it, kid. We don't have all the facts, which is why I've pulled some strings and arranged to get us into the CIA to see them," Hammett said.

Jonathan's eyes widened. "The Central Intelligence Agency?!"

"More like the Central Intelligence-*less* Agency!" Hammett barked. "Those clowns couldn't solve a game of Clue!"

"But they're in charge of my parents' case?"

"No, kid. We're in charge. We might live just north of Dumb and just east of Incompetent when it comes to books and numbers, but espionage we can handle!"

41

TOP SECRET

"My teacher asked me to describe myself in one word. I said 'alive.'"

—Harold Edmington, 11, Nova Scotia, Canada

SECURE DOCUMENTS

CHAPTER 4

<098762-HE-LOUC-101>

OCTOBER 30, 11:44 P.M. CENTRAL INTELLI-
GENCE AGENCY. LANGLEY, VIRGINIA

Why is it so hot in here? Jonathan thought as he
wiped the sweat from his brow. He wanted to open
a window, but there weren't any. The hallway was
narrow but long. The walls, institution gray, were
empty except for the interruption of a few beige
doors. Track lighting showered the space in a yel-
lowish tint that left Jonathan, Shelley, and Hammett looking more than a little jaundiced. Surreal.
There was no other word Jonathan could think of

to describe the situation. What had happened to the dull existence of Jonathan Murray? Afternoons spent staring at the wall or asking his parents to please turn down the sound on their video game. Sure, he had always thought his life boring beyond measure. But now he kind of missed it. The stability of boredom—the sense that he knew what was coming each day.

The sound of a door opening drew Jonathan's attention to the end of the hall. A woman, about fifty, in an oversized navy pantsuit appeared. *That's one tough-looking lady*, Jonathan thought as he watched her march toward them. She reminded him of a wrestler he had once seen on television: a woman whose signature move was pouncing on top of her opponents until they passed out.

Hammett narrowed his eyes, flared his nostrils, and coolly grumbled, "Agent O'Keefe."

"So this is the traitors' spawn?" she snarled, looking Jonathan up and down, taking in everything from his scuffed sneakers to the loose thread hanging from the collar of his shirt.

"I've never been so jealous in my life," Shelley muttered. "I would kill for that kind of nickname."

Hammett shook his head. "Keep it together, doll. This isn't about you."

"Exactly!" Shelley huffed. "I'm just the *friend* of the traitors' spawn! What a lame claim to fame."

"Where are my parents?" Jonathan asked Agent O'Keefe, nervously slipping his hands in and out of the pockets of his khaki trousers.

"What's your name?" the agent asked.

"Jonathan."

"My name's Jennifer O'Keefe and one day I'm going to call on you to testify against those people you call parents. And you may not believe it now, but when that day comes, you're going to say yes," she announced calmly. "The truth has a way of changing people."

"Enough with the chitchat. Where are they?" Hammett interrupted.

"You have ten minutes," Agent O'Keefe said, motioning to a nearby door.

OCTOBER 31, 1:02 A.M. CIA INTERROGA-TION ROOM. LANGLEY, VIRGINIA

Mickey and Carmen Murray sat side by side at a small wooden table. Soda cans and crumpled candy wrappers were strewn across the floor. Light beige walls, speckled with years' worth of stains, surrounded them. This was an interrogation room, a place where countless criminals before them had come to face the bleak reality of their lives. And yet, the Murrays appeared upbeat, almost happy. Did they understand they were at the CIA? That they had been arrested for treason? Did they even know what treason was? These were the questions that flitted through Jonathan's mind upon spotting his parents, both smiling widely.

"Mom! Dad!" Jonathan called out while running toward them, arms extended.

Pulling them into a group hug, Jonathan once again fought the urge to cry. Not because he was embarrassed, but rather, he knew it would distract from what they needed to do—save the Murrays.

"Champ! What are you doing here?" Mickey asked, pushing his shaggy blond hair behind his ears.

"What am I doing here? What are *you* doing here?" Jonathan asked pointedly.

Carmen shook her head and sighed. "I knew we forgot to tell you something."

"It's not Mom's fault; alien trackers are obsessed with secrecy. They kept reminding us not to tweet about them," Mickey said, rolling his eyes. "Like we know how to use Twitter!"

"Alien trackers?" Jonathan, Hammett, and Shelley repeated in unison.

"Yes!" Carmen said as she thrust both arms up in the air as if in the throes of a cheer routine. "Dad and I were recruited to work for the Alien Intelligence Agency. Pretty impressive, huh?"

"Wait! Aliens are real?!" Shelley said, grabbing hold of Jonathan's arm. "You know what

47

that means, don't you? We're even less special than before!"

Hammett snapped his fingers. "Listen up, folks, and listen up good!"

"Not to be rude," Mickey interrupted, "but aren't you a little old to be friends with Jonathan?"

"I'm not Jonathan's friend, Mr. Murray, I'm the private detective he hired to help you guys. So what do you say you two give me the facts and give 'em to me fast."

"Okay, well, my name is Carmen Lucia Murray and I was born on June twentieth—"

"Not about you! About what happened! Why are you in the big house? What did you do?" Hammett asked as he paced around the room, toothpick dangling from the corner of his mouth.

"It all started one afternoon when Carm and I were playing Surfing Zombies and these two teenagers showed up at the door. At first we thought they were selling Girl Scout cookies and we were like 'Heck yeah!' We love us some Thin Mints."

"But it turns out, they work for the Alien Intelligence Agency," Carmen added as she pulled something from her pocket. "They even gave us their card."

ALIEN INTELLIGENCE AGENCY

AIA

"Just because it walks like a human and talks like a
human, doesn't mean it's a human."*
*Full disclosure: 99.9% of the time it's a human.

"They needed our help to catch aliens masquerading as humans," Mickey explained proudly. "We had to get them this one file—a list of every undercover alien on Earth."

Jonathan's eyes widened as a lightbulb went off in his head. His parents had spent their lives reading comic books, watching science-fiction movies, and playing video games, thereby making a visit from the Alien Intelligence Agency seem within the realm of possibility to them. But then that small nagging voice returned. The one Jonathan had fought so hard to silence. What if his parents were acting? What if this was all a ruse to maintain their covers?

Who were these people he called Mom and Dad—lovable idiots or international operatives?

"So we went to Fred's house—" Mickey continued.

"Wait, who's Fred?" Hammett asked.

"A poodle," Mickey replied. "He's blind in one eye and smells like musty clothes, but he poops on command, and that's a big deal in our world."

"I can imagine," Hammett responded stiffly before motioning for Mickey to continue.

"The girls gave us two slips of paper. One with the computer's password and one with the file name. But we lost the scrap of paper with the file name on the way there."

"And all we could remember was that it was short and started with an *s*," Carmen chimed in. "So it took us a while to find the right one."

"You know what sounds really good right now?" Mickey said while staring off into space.

"Life in prison?" Shelley muttered under her breath.

"A burrito with extra guacamole."

"Yes!" Carmen responded. "Let's order delivery!"

Hammett pulled the toothpick from his mouth,

stepped toward the Murrays, and grumbled, "You've been arrested for treason—you don't get to order delivery!"

"Harsh," Mickey mumbled.

"Seriously," Carmen agreed.

Jonathan stared at his mother, flashes of his childhood flitting through his mind. This was the woman who had taught him—albeit incorrectly—how to tie his shoelaces. The woman who had pushed a candle into a cupcake to celebrate his birthday every year or so (Carmen Murray had never been very good with details like dates). Jonathan leaned in until he was mere inches from her face. He noted the wrinkles that crept away from her eyes. The scar on her left nostril that looked more like an enlarged pore than the last trace of a nose ring. The bronze color of her skin that darkened around the mouth. Jonathan recognized it all. But did that mean he knew her? Was she his mother or a stranger? Or both?

"Mom," Jonathan said before turning to his father. "Dad...please just tell me the truth. I might not be the smartest kid in the class or be able to run around the track without wheezing, but in this area, as crazy as it sounds, I can help you. But you have to tell me what really happened."

"I told you we should have told him!" Mickey snapped at Carmen before turning to Jonathan. "We always planned on telling you about the money."

"What money?" Jonathan asked as Hammett and Shelley stepped closer.

"The money from the African prince," Carmen answered.

"The African prince?" Jonathan repeated.

"He left us a million dollars in his will. Pretty cool, huh?" Mickey added with a confident smile. "I've already picked out a new surfboard. And a skateboard. And a television—"

"Wait, why would an African prince leave you even one dollar, let alone a million dollars?" Jonathan interrupted. "That makes no sense."

"May I interject?" Shelley said before clearing her throat. "Mr. and Mrs. Murray, did this African prince's lawyer contact you by e-mail?"

"Yes."

"Did he or she ask you for any personal information?"

"No . . . well, except for our Social Security numbers, dates of birth, mothers' maiden names, and our bank account number," Mickey answered.

"If I had a dollar for every time someone told me they'd been contacted by an African prince, I'd have two dollars. Or technically only one, since the other couple didn't tell me, I just saw them on the news."

Hammett grabbed Jonathan's arm and pulled him to the other side of the room. "Good news, kid. It's looking more and more likely that your parents are just a couple of dimwits who were used as pawns."

Jonathan smiled. The world suddenly made sense again.

"But the people who used your parents," Hammett continued, "the people they sent the STS file to...we don't know who they are, but there's little doubt they're going to use the map of the tunnels for nefarious purposes."

"Nefarious?" Jonathan asked, unsure what the word even meant.

"Criminal, evil..."

"What about Fred the poodle's owners? Maybe they know something."

"Fred the poodle's mother is a secretary for the Nuclear Planning Committee and his father is an executive for the Scholastic Aptitude Test, also known as the college entrance exam," Hammett explained. "We believe they targeted Fred's mother because of her dreadful organizational skills....She didn't even know she had a copy of the STS on her computer until your parents stole it."

Whack!

The door to the small room flung open, loudly banging into the wall.

"Time's up!" Agent O'Keefe announced, marching into the room.

"We've still got three minutes," Jonathan argued as he stared at his watch. "Or two minutes...no, wait..."

"Telling time's never been his thing," Shelley explained to the agent. "Actually, to be honest, nothing's ever really been his thing."

"What's that?" Jonathan asked Agent O'Keefe, noting the paper dangling from her left hand.

"This is what we call a bureaucratic waste of money," the woman answered as she held up a drawing of two teenage girls. "My boss brought in a sketch artist on the off chance these two were actually telling the truth."

Hammett grabbed the paper. His face blanched. His chin quivered. His eyes twitched. The toothpick fell from the corner of his mouth. His left leg started to tremble uncontrollably, much like a dog whose stomach was being scratched.

"Hammett, are you okay? Should I call a doctor?" Jonathan asked.

"No," Hammett said quietly as the tremors slowed.

"Is there a problem, Hammett?" Agent O'Keefe probed as she stepped closer.

"You could say that."

Agent O'Keefe smirked. "No one ever said defending traitors was easy."

"They're not traitors."

Rolling her eyes, Agent O'Keefe remarked, "Don't tell me you believe in aliens?"

"No. But I do believe in the Order of Merium."

"Does daydreaming count as an
extracurricular activity?"

—Akbar Khodaddi, 11, Madison, Wisconsin

CHAPTER 5

<098762-PM-LOUC-101>

OCTOBER 31, 1:48 A.M. CIA INTERROGA-
TION ROOM. LANGLEY, VIRGINIA

Shelley craned her neck, stepped onto her tiptoes, and widened her eyes as she stared at Hammett. So contorted and awkward was the small girl, Hammett thought she might be in the throes of a terrible muscle spasm brought on by a lack of potassium. *This kid needs a banana*, he thought, just as Shelley parted her lips and whispered, "Did you say the Order of Merium?"

Hammett nodded.

"Man, I wish I had a burrito," Mickey mumbled, still seated next to Carmen at the table in the center of the room.

"Dad! You have bigger problems than Mexican food!" Jonathan said before turning to Hammett. "What's the Order of Merium? And how does Shelley know about it?"

"Johno, Johno, Johno," Shelley said, shaking her head. "You clearly wasted your education on useless stuff like multiplication and geography, but not me, Johno. Not me."

Jonathan rolled his eyes and wiped the sweat from his forehead. If ever there was a time he wasn't in the mood for a Shelley-ism, it was now. But experience had taught him it was easier to let her talk than to try to stop her.

Shelley adjusted her glasses as she did anytime she wanted to emphasize her words. *I'm reminding people that I'm smart*, she thought. *Smart people wear glasses*. Never mind that she had met tons of dolts in glasses and geniuses with perfect vision; this was Shelley's theory and she was sticking to it.

"The Order of Merium is a band. Very cutting-edge. I would describe their sound as something along the lines of pregnant dolphins crying out for food…with a light drum track in the background."

Hammett looked at Shelley and smiled. She might be deluded, but she sure did know how to spin a tale.

"The Order of Merium is *actually* a secret society located in the western part of Bulgaria," Hammett explained. "They have nation status, meaning that Bulgarian authorities have no power on their soil."

Jonathan clenched his jaw and grumbled, "But who are they?"

Hammett swallowed audibly and then answered, "They're the people who rule the world."

"I still don't understand!" Jonathan replied as Shelley opened her mouth to say something. "Not now, Shells! Not now!"

"Listen here, kiddos, and listen good. What I'm about to say is the truth. But as you know, the truth can be scary. Real scary."

"Scarier than your parents being arrested for treason?" Jonathan blurted out, his tone harsh, his face covered in sweaty splotches.

"You're like a caterpillar becoming a butterfly right now...an angry butterfly....Do those exist?" Shelley trailed off as Hammett grabbed Jonathan by the shoulders and began speaking so close to his face that the boy could smell the stale coffee on his breath.

"For over a hundred years there have been rumors that the Order of Merium has been cheating and stealing its way into positions of power so that its members can manipulate stock markets, businesses, laws, pretty much society as a whole....Bottom line, if they wanted the STS file, they're planning something big against the US government."

"Hold on," Carmen Murray interrupted. "Are you saying that the girls weren't from the Alien Intelligence Agency?"

"There is no Alien Intelligence Agency! You were conned into committing treason!" Jonathan answered.

"And that's not a good thing, right?"

"No, Mom, it's not a good thing," Jonathan replied, and then released an epically long sigh.

"How could you tell from the sketch that they

60

were from the Order of Merium?" Shelley asked. "Wait, don't tell me...you had a psychic flash....I get them too....For instance, right now I sense Jonathan is thinking about buying more khaki slacks online."

"Not even close."

"Look at these girls," Hammett said as he held up the sketch. "Well groomed, smiling. They look like any other high school students until you look a bit closer. Each one has three moles arranged in a triangle under her left eye."

"So the girls are related?" Jonathan asked. "They both inherited the same moles?"

"They're not moles; they're tattoos."

"Kids getting tattoos? And to think my parents were scandalized when I pierced my ears," Shelley muttered.

"It's how members recognize each other out in the world. Within the Order, everyone must wear a mask and cloak."

"Hammett?" Agent O'Keefe interrupted. "As much as I've enjoyed this session of creative writing, I've got prisoners to process."

Hammett scowled. "They're under arrest; they're not prisoners. There's a difference."

"It's just a matter of time. They're guilty and they're gonna go down...hard."

Hammett offered Agent O'Keefe a steely look before stating, "They're telling the truth."

"That's the funny thing about the truth: Nothing's true unless you can prove it."

"Then we'll prove it," Jonathan announced, his voice steady and sure.

Hammett nodded as he pulled out his cell phone, an old flip phone held together by tape and a couple of stickers stolen from the post office.

"What's that?" Shelley asked.

"It's my cell phone. It was one of the first models on the market. It's got lousy reception and there's always a buzzing noise, but no one can trace it," Hammett explained as he finished dialing and put the phone to his ear. "Maidenkirk, get the Dark Bird. We're heading to Bulgaria....No, absolutely not...that boy cannot come....Tell Carl the answer is NO!"

OCTOBER 31, 3:32 A.M. AIRSTRIP. NORTHERN VIRGINIA

Standing in the middle of an empty field lined with trees wrapped in shadows, Jonathan grabbed hold of Shelley's hand. He squeezed it tightly as the wind ripped past them, whistling. They shivered. It was the cold air, the lack of sleep, and the rush of adrenaline all mixed together.

"Shells, do you think we'll actually be able to pull this off?"

"Of course, Johno! We're awesome. We saved the vice president. We saved England from a virus that could have made the whole country dumb. We can easily save your parents. We just have to make it to Bulgaria, sneak into the secret society, find the girls who tricked them, and then make it out alive before the society uses the information your parents gave them to ruin the US government."

"That sounds really hard."

"That's because you have normal ears. But not me, Johno. Not me. I have what are known as selective ears.... They only hear what they want to hear ... and right now they want to hear that we are going to succeed!"

"Don't take this the wrong way, but that explains a lot—"

"It's here!" Shelley interrupted. "The Dark Bird has landed!"

"Should I be offended that my sister tells people she's an only child?"

—Susan Ishere, 12, Columbia, California

CHAPTER 6

OCTOBER 31, 3:34 A.M. AIRSTRIP. NORTHERN VIRGINIA

From the edge of the forest emerged a World War II transport plane. Swathed in darkness, the silhouette of the aircraft—two propellers and a deep body that appeared much like the bottom of a boat held upright by two wings—moved slowly toward Jonathan and Shelley.

"What's that sound?" Jonathan asked.

Clink-clunk-clack. Clink-clunk-clack.

The plane crept out of the shadow of the trees and into the silver light of the moon.

Jonathan's mouth dropped open. "Oh no… no…no…no way…."

"Oh come on, Johno…it's not *that bad*."

"The plane's held together by rope and masking tape!"

A rusted metal bar snapped off the tail of the aircraft as Shelley and Jonathan noticed that none other than Nurse Maidenkirk was in the cockpit.

"Okay, it *is* that bad," Shelley admitted.

As the rusty black plane sputtered to a stop, the back hatch lowered and Hammett jumped out.

"Come on, kids, don't just stand there! Move your stompers! We've got an eighteen-hour flight ahead of us!"

"Eighteen hours?" Shelley repeated.

"The Dark Bird needs to stop for refueling a few times, plus, she's an old lady. And you can't rush an old lady."

"We're going to spend eighteen hours in that thing?" Jonathan asked as he sized up the screws and bolts, so old and rusted they appeared to be disintegrating right before his eyes.

"The Dark Bird sure is a gem, isn't she?" Hammett answered.

"Only if by *gem*, you mean death trap," Jonathan muttered.

"Hammy," Shelley chimed in, "as you know, I'm an optimist, a glass-half-full kind of kid. While Johno here is more of a glass-half-empty—or actually, on second thought, more of a glass-has-poisonous-water—type of kid, but even I have to agree with him about this contraption!"

"The Dark Bird might look like a heap of junk, and for that reason we store her at the demolition yard on the other side of those trees there," Hammett said as he pointed behind him. "But that's her disguise. When military officials see the Dark Bird, they laugh. They think, *Some old coot is taking his heap of garbage out for a spin.*"

"I guess what we're trying to say is, we're worried the disguise is a little *too real*," Jonathan responded as he pointed to the rope that held the left wing in place.

"After everything we've been through, you don't trust me?" Hammett asked, looking down at his shoes.

"No, of course we do," Jonathan answered right away.

"Good," Hammett said as he looked up. "Then get in."

"We may trust you, but we definitely don't trust Nurse Maidenkirk as the pilot," Shelley said, pointing to the cockpit window.

"You've got a point there, doll. But Maidenkirk was the only pilot available. And, frankly, we don't have the time to find someone else. Not if we stand a chance at saving the Murrays."

Jonathan nodded as he stepped toward the back hatch. "Shells, I think it's best if you stay here. I'll be okay on my own."

"Johno, I'm the ketchup to your French fry. The

maraschino cherry to your sundae. Without me, you're just not as good," Shelley said, climbing onto the plane.

OCTOBER 31, 6:58 P.M. EASTERN STANDARD TIME. THE DARK BIRD. SOMEWHERE BE-TWEEN WASHINGTON, DC, AND BULGARIA

Jonathan, Shelley, and Hammett sat next to each other on one of two benches that lined the metal walls of the plane. No traditional seats. No windows. Just dangling wires, rusty bolts, and a pile of green duffel bags.

Clink-clack-buzz-clink-clack-buzz.

"Is the engine supposed to make that sound?" Jonathan asked as he took in his surroundings.

"Of course it is, kid; it's all part of the disguise," Hammett said as he popped a new toothpick into his mouth.

"The plane is kind of like Charl...hidden in plain sight...pun intended," Shelley said with a smile. "Get it, *plain* sight? And I'm talking about a *plane*?"

"I hate puns almost as much as I hate this plane," Jonathan grumbled to himself.

Hammett shook his head. "I don't know what to do with Carl. He's got natural talent—his skin allows him to blend into almost anything—"

"If I were a serial killer, I'd try to turn him into an outfit," Shelley interrupted, thinking about the boy's spotted skin before shuddering at her own comment. "Wow, sorry about that, guys.... That really crossed the line."

"There's a line?"

"Not a well-marked one, Johno. But yes, there's a line."

"Carl has the potential to be the best operative this division's ever seen if we can just get him to shape up. The kid's got no follow-through. He never finishes anything! He doesn't even bother to empty his whole bladder when he goes to the bathroom!"

Jonathan recoiled. "I'm afraid to ask, but how do you know that?"

"Carl told me. That's the other thing about him. He can't keep a secret to save his life!" Hammett said. "He's the kind of kid who would just walk out in the middle of a mission and sit in a park and then return with some story about sleeping in a McDonald's for three days."

"If I weren't a part-time vegetarian, I would live in a McDonald's. I love that potato smell," Shelley added. "Like if they made it into a perfume, I'd buy it."

"If you're a part-time vegetarian, then you shouldn't eat the fries, at least part-time. They contain natural beef flavor," a voice came from the floor—the green duffel bags, to be exact.

"No!!!" Hammett screamed, jumping to his feet.

"Oh, hey, Hammett," Carl said as he stood up.

"Not again!" Hammett shouted as he stomped toward the cockpit. "Maidenkirk!"

"Did I ever tell you about the time I met the real Santa Claus at a mall in Minneapolis?" Carl asked. "I was with my grandma, who loves to hang out with old people, so she asked him if he was free for dinner.... They split a pizza in the food court.... Now Santa's my grandpa."

"Lucky you," Shelley droned as she and Jonathan stared at Carl.

"Not really. Turns out Santa's super-grumpy.... My grandma says it's because he's unemployed most of the year."

Jonathan nodded, resisting the urge to "correct" Carl, to tell him that the guy who married his grandmother wasn't really Santa, that should Santa actually exist, he's not spending his free time at the food court at the mall. But in the end, did it really matter to Jonathan what Carl believed? No. Plus, a part of Jonathan was envious; what a luxury to worry about a grumpy grandfather who may or may not be Santa rather than the arrest of your parents for treason!

Carl motioned to the plane's cabin. "Did you know we're surrounded by people? *Invisible* people."

Shelley lowered her glasses, peering over the rims at Carl. "Are you telling me that we're surrounded by ghosts?"

"I don't know if they're ghosts. I just know they're invisible."

"But you can see them?" Jonathan asked.

"Of course I can't see them—they're invisible!"

"Then how do you know they're here?" Jonathan continued.

Carl smiled. "That's the question."

"No, that's my question to you," Jonathan clarified.

"And that's my question to the universe."

Crawling out of the cockpit, Hammett announced loudly, "Carl, you aren't going on the mission! You hear me? You might have snuck onto the Dark Bird, but this is where your trip's going to end."

"Sure," Carl said, winking at Hammett and then turning toward Jonathan and Shelley.

"Hammett loves to mess with me, kind of like my mom. She's always playing around with me—putting spiders in my lunch, invisible *h*'s in my name—"

"Your mom put a spider in your lunch?" Shelley asked.

"She said it crawled in there on its own, but I know better."

Shelley nodded, rubbed her chin, and asked, "What school do you go to?"

"Mostly John Adams, but sometimes I forget and go to Lincoln Heights too."

"Four hours!" Nurse Maidenkirk shouted from the cockpit.

"Thank heavens there's only four hours left until we land," Jonathan said as he picked up a pair of binoculars and motioned for Shelley to tuck them into her backpack.

"Who said anything about *landing*?" Hammett answered.

Jonathan's eyes widened. "Excuse me?"

"Listen, kid, there's only one surefire way into the Order of Merium: parachuting. But there's no need to worry. It's kind of like riding a bike, only you're in the sky and a lot more likely to die."

"Then how is it like riding a bike?"

"It's not, kid. I was just trying to calm your nerves."

"The first jump's always the hardest," Shelley said as she placed her hand on Jonathan's shoulder.

Jonathan rolled his eyes. "Sure, Shells. Because you've done it before?"

"No, but I have been pushed out of a Ferris wheel by my sister, so I'm pretty sure I know what to expect."

"Your sister pushed you out of a Ferris wheel?" Jonathan asked, his face growing whiter and pastier by the second.

"It was pretty close to the ground," Shelley explained. "I think it had something to do with me decapitating her favorite doll."

Hammett snapped and clipped Jonathan and Shelley into their gear, which looked a bit like a backpack attached to a dog's harness. After double-checking that the parachutes were properly packed, he handed them pocket-sized copies of *How to Make Great Popcorn in the Microwave.*

"Everything we know about the Order of Merium is in here," Hammett said as he pushed a button, lowering the back hatch of the plane.

"That's it? That's all the preparation we're getting?" Jonathan screeched, his anxiety growing exponentially.

Hammett nodded. "If you remember to pull the cord and roll when you land, you probably won't break too many bones."

Jonathan looked at Shelley sitting next to him; she was smiling. How could she smile at a time like this? But then he remembered Shelley had the ability to tune out reality and only hear what she wanted to. He still couldn't believe that he was in this situation—literally seconds from jumping out of a plane with little to no training. He had always thought of himself as an old beige minivan that smelled of stale Cheerios and spilled coffee. But as he stood up and moved to the back of the plane, the cold wind hitting his face, he realized that wasn't true. Not anymore. *Forget the minivan*, he thought, *I'm a sports car now. A red one.*

Jonathan jumped first, free-falling through the black sky before pulling the cord, opening his parachute, and instantly slowing his descent.

Maybe this won't be so hard after all, Jonathan thought just as a familiar voice called out from above.

"Help me! Someone help me!"

TOP SECRET

"I asked my dad whether
someone might want to clone me
one day. He shook his head and
said, 'Your brother, maybe, but
you? No way.'"

—Anthony Johnson, 10, Minneapolis,
Minnesota

SECURE
DOCUMENTS

CHAPTER 7

<098762-PM-LOUC-101>

NOVEMBER 1, 5:43 A.M. THE SKY OVER BULGARIA

Shelley's voice cut through Jonathan. His body jittered. His eyes bulged. His throat constricted. Utterly powerless to help his friend, his mind raced. Was it Shelley's parachute? Did it fail to open? Was her body about to flash past him, spiraling to a sudden death? *Slap!* That's the sound her body would make as it hit the ground. Maybe he could catch her? Were his arms long enough? Would she fall within grabbing distance? *Wait*, he thought. If there were something wrong with Shelley's parachute, he would know by now; she would have already sped by. After all, he was floating down at an almost leisurely pace. Jonathan looked up, his view completely blocked by the large black parachute. So concerned was he about Shelley, he had momentarily forgotten that he was on a mission, that he would soon be landing in the Order of Merium. And that there, within the walls of the secret society, lay his parents' fate.

Looking down, Jonathan noticed that the wind was pushing him off course. As he drifted farther and farther from the walled grounds of the Order of Merium, a voice suddenly ripped through the night.

"Khaki!"

Straight ahead, on course for the garden, was Shelley. Or at least he assumed that it was Shelley, for much like when the Dark Bird came out of the forest, he could only decipher the silhouette of the parachute and person.

"You're not going to make it!" Shelley screamed. "Use the cords to steer!"

I can't fail before I've even started, can I? Jonathan wondered. *Yes, of course you can! You're Jonathan Murray—you still don't know if midnight is twelve a.m. or twelve p.m.! Do something, do anything, just save yourself,* Jonathan thought as he grabbed the cords and began pulling at them haphazardly. Left. Right. More left. Less left. More right.

"What are you doing?" Shelley screeched as she wafted to the ground.

What am I doing? Why do I never *know what I'm doing?* Jonathan thought. *Pay attention! Focus!* Gently pulling the left cord, Jonathan moved back toward the Order of Merium. But then he worried he might pass over it, so he tugged at the right cord. Back and forth he went, coming closer and closer to the ground with every second. So busy was the boy steering, he completely forgot Hammett's instructions to roll upon landing, instead performing what looked like a cannonball meets belly flop onto the grass. An ungracious arrival to be sure, but he was alive and uninjured.

"Shells? Shells?" Jonathan whispered as he found his way out from under the silky black parachute.

Standing over Jonathan, hands on hips and glasses sliding off the tip of her nose, was Shelley. And she did not look pleased.

"Are you okay?! I heard you scream, but I couldn't see anything!"

"Have you ever heard of pheromones?" Shelley asked as she pushed up her glasses. "It's a scent animals release causing other animals to either love them or hate them."

"I'm afraid of what's going to come out of your mouth next."

"It appears my pheromones are irresistible, because I now have *not one, but two* stalkers," Shelley said as she turned and pulled Carl away from the bush he was using as a disguise. "Seconds before jumping, Charl grabbed me and pushed us both out of the plane."

"It's true," Carl added. "We hugged the whole way down so I wouldn't die."

"Sadly, that is accurate.... We hugged... hard....
I wanted to let go many, many times, mostly due
to his personality, but I didn't," Shelley said before
looking down and shaking her head.

"Wait, who's the second stalker?" Jonathan
asked as he stood up.

Shelley gave Jonathan a long and meaningful
look.

"I'm your partner!"

Shelley shrugged. "Some might say that's the
perfect cover."

Jonathan pushed the hair from his forehead and
took in his surroundings for the first time since landing. Rising in the east, the sun cast a golden glow
over the garden. Thick, stumpy trees with blossom-
ing white flowers filled the air with a sweet, almost
saccharine scent. The grass, unkempt and limp, felt
like wet carpet, water seeping through with each
step. And all around them a stone wall soared,
almost twenty feet high, covered in dark green moss.
The grounds, the territory of the Order of Merium,
formed a near-perfect circle. And placed squarely
at the center, among the trees and slushy greenery,
was the castle. Columns lined the limestone structure

with stained-glass windows and black wrought iron bars. Turrets marked each of the castle's four corners.

"According to *How to Make Great Popcorn in the Microwave*, the Order maintains a contrary schedule, sleeping during the day and waking at night," Jonathan said as he read Hammett's notes. "Which means this is the perfect time to find the girls."

"Then what?" Carl asked.

"What do you mean?" Jonathan replied.

"Once we find them, what do we do?" Carl pressed on.

"We take them back to the United States with us," Jonathan answered.

"How are we going to do that?" Carl asked.

"I don't know," Jonathan admitted.

"You mean you don't have a plan?!" Carl remarked, throwing his hands in the air.

"We're unexceptionals; we never have plans! Not good ones, anyway!" Jonathan answered.

"Not having a plan seems like a really bad plan...maybe even the worst plan," Carl muttered.

Shelley pursed her lips and stomped her left foot. "Darn it! Charl is right! We need a plan!"

"The *h* is silent, remember?"

"We don't actually need the girls; we just need evidence. A videotaped confession? A handwritten letter? Something, anything we can take with us," Jonathan said as he looked from Carl to Shelley.

"I'm on it, Colonel, and by *Colonel*, I mean friend with no military experience," Shelley said as she saluted Jonathan. "By the time we're done with the Order of Merium, those girls are going to be crying, begging us for forgiveness! *Please forgive us, Shelltastic!*"

"Shelltastic?" Carl repeated.

"It's my nickname."

"Really? Then why doesn't Jerry call you that?"

"My name is Jonathan, like Jonathan...Why are there no famous people named Jonathan?!" the boy lamented.

Shelley narrowed her eyes and thoughtfully responded, "As a wise child, or perhaps just a very short adult, once told me while waiting in line for the bathroom at the mall, *We don't get to pick our parents or our names, but at least the latter can be changed with twenty-five dollars and your mom's forged signature.*"

Jonathan had stopped listening, as he so often did when Shelley spoke. He was too busy staring at the columns lining the building. They reminded him of a jail, just like the one that his parents would soon be whiling away the rest of their days in. This was it. This was his only chance of saving them. The people who not only gave him life but love, and of course, daily meals with little to no nutritional value.

"Vending machines," Jonathan muttered to himself, remembering his parents' answer when asked to name their favorite food group.

"What was that?"

"Nothing," Jonathan replied to Shelley, turning toward the castle's large wooden door. "Come on, let's do this."

NOVEMBER 1, 7:54 A.M. HALLWAY. THE ORDER OF MERIUM

Creeping down the dark hallway, Jonathan, Shelley, and Carl noted the antiquities: armor, wall tapestries, swords, a miniature cannon.

"This place smells like an old fish tank," Shelley said as she buried her nose inside her shirt. "Which reminds me of Mitch...poor sweet Mitch..."

"Who's Mitch?" Carl asked.

"Only the greatest cat that ever lived. He was a tabby. And when he died I used my old fish tank as a coffin.... It smelled terrible."

"Did you kill Mitch?"

"No, I didn't kill Mitch! Part-time vegetarians don't kill pets!"

"Just in case you forgot," Jonathan whispered tensely, "we're here to find the girls, get some evidence, and get out! We're not here to share our favorite stories about dead pets and makeshift coffins!"

Shelley nodded as Carl bumped into a table, knocking off a lamp in the process. With less than a second to spare, Jonathan dove to the floor, using his body to break the lamp's fall. Red in the face, back muscles throbbing, Jonathan carefully stood up and returned the lamp to the table.

"Sorry about that," Carl muttered.

"Do not touch anything," Jonathan said, his cheeks flushed with anger. "Do not make any loud noises. Unless, of course, you want to spend the next seven decades locked in a dungeon!"

TOP SECRET

"I must have had a really exciting past life. It's the only explanation I can come up with for why this one's so boring."

—Raha Shaw, 12, Woodland Hills, California

★ SECURE ★
DOCUMENTS

CHAPTER 8

<098762-PM-LOUC-101>

NOVEMBER 1, 8:04 A.M. HALLWAY. THE
ORDER OF MERIUM

This is *worse* than an old fish tank, Shelley thought
as she tiptoed down the corridor after Jonathan.
Like clothes left in the washing machine overnight,
the scent was musty, mildewy, hamster-esque. *Why
does the smell remind me of hamsters?* she wondered. Maybe she tried to clean her hamster in the
washing machine and it came out a stinky damp
mess? Can hamsters survive the spin cycle? Was
she a hamster assassin? No! She would remember

that, Shelley assured herself. Death is a hard thing to forget.

Death ... the word lingered in her mind. Was this a psychic flash, a premonition of things to come? Were they going to die in the Order of Merium?

"Johno!" Shelley whispered frantically.

"What?"

Staring into Jonathan's brown eyes, Shelley suddenly froze. Most kids her age had a handful of friends, but prior to Jonathan she had exactly one— a goldfish named Zelda. And though the fish had always been loyal (full disclosure: Zelda lived in a bowl and therefore couldn't leave even if she wanted to), she lacked many of the characteristics that made friendships work—the ability to talk, live on land, etc. No, it wasn't until Jonathan that Shelley learned what life was like with a friend. *Better.* That was what came to mind when Shelley thought of Jonathan—he made life better. So how could she desert him now, when he needed her most? The answer was simple— she couldn't. And so instead of screaming, *We're about to die, we need to get out of here*, she looked around and casually asked, "Have you seen Charl?"

Just then the boy stepped out from a tapestry hanging on the wall and waved. "Hey, guys."

Jonathan narrowed his eyes as an idea formed. "Were you hiding?"

Carl nodded. "Don't take it personally, but I don't have a lot of faith in your plan and I really want to live...because I like being alive...and because I bought a year's worth of sunscreen and I really want to use it...."

A figure flashed before them, scurrying down the corridor that bisected the hall where they stood. He was tall and plump. His limbs wobbled and jutted out when he moved. A frenetic energy emanated from the boy so clearly that Jonathan and Shelley only had to look at him to feel it. Thick glasses bounced up and down on his nose while his frizzy brown hair, a style best described as "electrocuted," framed his round face.

Frozen with fear, Jonathan and Shelley both silently hoped the boy didn't look in their direction. And then, just as he was about to vanish from sight, the boy turned and retraced his steps down the hall as though he had forgotten something. The sound of his feet brushing against the carpet sent chills up Jonathan's spine. If they were caught now, without a single ounce of evidence to exonerate the Murrays, it was over.

Back and forth the boy went, buzzing like a bee, until he finally disappeared down the corridor.

"I thought you said the Order of Merium slept during the day," Shelley whispered to Jonathan.

"That's what it said in *How to Make Great Popcorn in the Microwave*," Jonathan said as he pulled out the book. "But it also says they wear cloaks and masks at all times and that the Order keeps a diary.... Who knows how accurate this information is?"

"Let's follow him," Shelley suggested. "I think we should see what he's up to."

NOVEMBER 1, 8:18 A.M. THE KITCHEN. THE ORDER OF MERIUM

Jonathan and Shelley peered around the corner, closely watching the pudgy boy, no more than fifteen, dash around the kitchen in a frenzy as he prepared food for the Order of Merium. Flour exploded into the air, dusting the appliances in a light snow. Eggs crashed to the stone floor. Milk dribbled off the counter. Pancakes burned. Smoke hung heavily in the air.

"Harold cook! Harold clean! Harold here! Harold there! Don't touch the black book, Harold! More pancakes, Harold! Move it, Harold! Harold! Harold! Harold!" the boy grumbled to himself as he moved around the kitchen.

"Supersloth Shelley strikes again," she whispered proudly in Jonathan's ear. "The kid's name is Harold."

"A sloth is an animal that moves really slowly. So if you're a supersloth it means you're really slow."

"No, it means I'm a detective."

"A sloth is a furry animal with long arms. A sleuth is a detective."

"I hate it when you know things," Shelley grunted as Harold took off his apron, rinsed his hands, and scampered out the back door of the kitchen.

Broken eggshells, scraggly lines of yolk drizzled across the countertops, and stacks of batter-encrusted bowls welcomed the trio as they tiptoed into the kitchen. Overwhelmed by the urge to clean up—a habit developed after years of living with messy, highly disorganized parents—Jonathan literally trembled.

"Pancakes!" Carl remarked as he pushed past Jonathan, knocking the boy against the stove. Steadying himself with his hands on the nearest surface, Jonathan whimpered, then dropped to the floor.

"What's wrong?" Shelley asked, kneeling beside her friend.

Red lines—burns—crisscrossed Jonathan's palms.

"Two grilled hands with a side of clumsy," Shelley remarked as they turned to watch Carl shove a pancake into his mouth before taking a swig of syrup straight from the bottle. "Well, there's no denying he's an unexceptional in the table manners department...."

"Speaking of which, I think Harold's the unexceptional of the Order of Merium," Jonathan said.

Shelley nodded. "In other words, not worth following."

"Exactly."

Creeping up a spiral staircase, Carl tapped Jonathan and Shelley on the shoulders. "Guys? I think
I'm going to head out."

Shelley whirled around, taken off guard by the
comment. "Head out where?"

"Back to the US...get some French fries on the
way....Those pancakes just didn't cut it for me."

"Charl, we haven't even figured out our escape
route yet, so there's no *heading out*, as you put it."

"I'm just not feeling this whole spy thing anymore...probably because I realized that *unexceptional* means you're not good at anything, so you
have really bad plans, which will most likely get me
killed, which will stop me from watching future sea-
sons of TV shows I'm really looking forward to."

"Charl, you joined this mission after Hammett
explicitly told you that you weren't ready," Shelley said as she grabbed his shirt and pulled him
closer.

"Which it turns out he was right about."

Shelley flushed with anger as Jonathan placed

his hand on her shoulder, hoping that the presence of his slightly maimed limb might remind her to keep her cool.

"And now you want to leave because you've realized we're *unexceptional*?"

Carl nodded. "That's pretty much it in a nutshell."

"I'm going to let you in on a little secret," Jonathan said as he forcibly removed Shelley's hand from Carl's shirt.

"I love secrets....I can't keep them, but I love hearing them...and repeating them."

"We don't care what you want to do. We don't care if you want to go home. We don't care if you want your teddy bear. We don't care if you want your mom. You are stuck on this mission because you decided to jump out of the Dark Bird with us. So whatever doubts you're feeling, get over them. Whatever question you have about our unexceptionalness, get over it. We've handled missions that would curl your toes—"

"In a scary way, not a muscle spasm kind of way," Shelley clarified.

"Really, Shells? I was sort of on a roll there."

"You were....I'm sorry....I'd like to take back that clarification...so let's just all pretend it never happened....I never said a thing...except of course for what I'm saying right now...or actually, I wouldn't have said this if I hadn't said that other thing earlier, so..."

Jonathan held up his hand, indicating that now was the appropriate time for Shelley to stop babbling. He then turned his attention back to Carl. "Bottom line: We don't care if you have doubts about our abilities—we're unexceptional and proud," he finished, his voice firm and assertive.

Shelley smiled at Carl and then motioned toward Jonathan. "I taught him everything he knows. Except how to dress...That's all him....I definitely don't want credit for that."

NOVEMBER 1, 11:14 A.M. HALLWAY. THE ORDER OF MERIUM

In and out of rooms the trio went, carefully scanning for some sign of the girls, or anyone, for that matter. Other than Harold, they had yet to come across another person.

Jonathan cracked open the door to what looked

like a library or study. A sliver of light cut through a small gap between the thick velvet curtains, faintly illuminating the room. Floor-to-ceiling bookshelves, stiff leather sofas, and a large table dominated the space.

"Over here," Shelley whispered, moving through the room. "It's a model of the Order of Merium."

It must be one-tenth of the size, or one-hundredth of the size, Shelley thought, before remembering that she didn't understand fractions and therefore should stick to general descriptions such as "small" or "little."

"Look down here," Jonathan said as his eyes went from the kitchen to the basement and finally to a series of tunnels. "I wonder where these lead."

"Forget the tunnels! Where do these people sleep?" Shelley remarked before excitedly snapping her fingers. "Look at all these teeny-tiny bunk beds."

Hunched over, angling for a closer view, Carl appeared unusually interested in the sleeping quarters. It was a marked change for the boy, who thus far had shown more interest in pancakes than the mission.

"I wonder where they got these little beds," Carl mumbled. "I'd love to buy a few for my chipmunks."

Shelley lowered her head and peered over the top of her glasses. "You have pet chipmunks?"

"When you spend as much time in trees and bushes as I do, you tend to make friends with the locals."

Shelley nodded as a twinge of jealousy took hold—befriending wildlife had long been on her to-do list. And while a baby kangaroo was her first choice, she would have been more than happy with a chipmunk or two.

As the chipmunk chatter continued, Jonathan focused in on the shape of the wall surrounding the Order of Merium—a perfect circle. How many homes, or castles, for that matter, were enclosed in a perfect circle? *Odd*, Jonathan thought. But then again, this was a secret society; maybe there was a reason for the shape? Jonathan's eyes moved from the wall to the front door. There, mounted on the stone surface, just to the left of the tall wooden gate, was a black lever. After running his finger over the lever a few times, he gently pushed down.

"Oh no…what have I done?" Jonathan mumbled

upon hearing what sounded like garbage trucks picking up cans.

"Wow," Shelley muttered as she watched a metal lattice emerge from inside the model's wall, rising over the top of the castle, creating a dome, and locking down onto the other side.

"Great," Jonathan sighed. "As if things weren't already hard enough…"

"If reincarnation exists, I'd like to put in a request to be smart in my next life."

—Angelina Leitfoot, 14, Pass Christian, Mississippi

CHAPTER 9

<098762-PM-LOUC-101>

NOVEMBER 1, 1:29 P.M. SLEEPING QUAR-
TERS. THE ORDER OF MERIUM

"They sleep in their cloaks? They must sweat a lot,"
Shelley whispered as the trio popped their heads
into the sleeping quarters—row upon row of bunk
beds, all filled with slumbering Meriums. "No wonder this place smells so bad."

"I hate to bring up the *p*-word again," Carl whispered. "But do we have a plan?"

"You and this *plan* obsession," Shelley scoffed,

shaking her head. "How many times do we have to tell you, unexceptionals don't have plans!"

"I have a plan," Jonathan interrupted.

"You have a plan? And you kept it from me? Charl I understand, but me? Shelltastic? I'm your partner in crime, only not crime, the opposite, actually.... Is spying the opposite of crime? Not really... I'd say it's more like justified criminal behavior...."

"This is the one time they have their masks off, right? When they're sleeping," Jonathan said, prompting Carl and Shelley to nod. "We need to mark the girls' cloaks in some way so we can identify them later."

Carl smiled. "Like with gold stars?"

"Do you have gold stars on you?" Shelley asked.

"No, but I'm kind of obsessed with them since I've never gotten one before. That's where my nickname comes from, 'Carl-no-star.'"

"We definitely can do better than that. I'm thinking Spots. What do you say, Khaki?"

"Wax."

"You want to call him Wax? Like earwax?"

"No, I want to use wax to mark the girls'

cloaks," Jonathan said as he removed a white candle from the sconce on the wall.

"What if someone wakes up?" Carl asked.

"Jump on top of them and cover their face with a pillow," Shelley said before pausing. "Actually, that might hurt them, and if they're hurt…"

"They can't testify," Jonathan interjected.

"That and, of course, we would have to add violent hooliganism to our résumé, which is an extracurricular not everyone understands," Shelley finished sarcastically.

Jonathan pulled out the sketch of the girls' faces and quietly made his way into the room. Peering from bed to bed, he quickly noted that everyone was sleeping on their backs, arms folded across their chests. One by one, they searched, all the while hoping that no one would wake up. *Sleep*, they thought, *please just stay asleep*. Nearing the back of the room, Jonathan threw his arm in the air, silently signaling the other two to come over. *It's her*, Jonathan mouthed as he pointed to one of the two girls in the sketch and then the bottom bunk.

Shelley looked at the girl and nodded. That was

definitely her. Jonathan dribbled hot wax along the hem of her long cloak as she slept. Once finished, he looked up at the top bunk and smiled—they had found the other girl. Desperate to be part of the action, Shelley grabbed the candle from Jonathan's hand and started up the ladder. However, finding it difficult to climb with one hand, she popped the long white candle between her teeth just like she had once seen an actor do with a knife in a film she could only vaguely remember. *What is that? What is that terrible smell? Ahh! No! Burning! My hair's on fire!* Shelley dropped the candle as she frantically slapped her head to put out the flames. Having let go of the ladder, she crashed to the floor with a thud, a loud thud. Jonathan picked up the candle, still burning, blew it out, and then did the only thing he could think of—he hid under the bed.

"Ugh, uh," the girl on the lower bunk moaned as she slowly woke up. "What was that?"

Looking around, Shelley suddenly realized that she was the sole member of the team out in the open, like a deer in the middle of a field during hunting season. As expected, Carl was nowhere to be found, but Jonathan? Where was Jonathan? Squeezed beneath the bottom bunk, he frantically motioned for Shelley to join him.

"Carol! Carol!" the girl on the lower bunk whispered. "Something's burning!"

Shelley slid under the bed next to Jonathan and covered her head with her sweatshirt in an effort to conceal the burned smell. *This is it*, Shelley thought, *my hair is going to bring us all down!*

"Glenda? What's the matter?" the girl from the top bunk whispered, hanging her head over the edge.

Staring at the lower bunk across from them, Shelley squinted, tilted her head, and then squinted some more. It couldn't be, she thought, Carl wasn't that dumb. And so she removed her glasses, carefully cleaned them with the bottom of her shirt, and then slipped them back on. But she could still see Carl stretched out next to the girl on the lower bunk. Who hides in the bed of one of the very people they are hiding from? Carl, that's who!

Shelley pointed to the bed across from them, but so good was Carl at blending that at first Jonathan didn't see him. It was only when the boy moved that Jonathan realized what he was looking at. *No, no, no!* Jonathan mouthed to Shelley.

"Something's burning," Glenda whispered to Carol. "Can't you smell it?"

"Maybe Harold got a bagel stuck in the toaster again?"

"Should we go yell at him?" Glenda suggested.

"I'm exhausted...." Carol replied.

"Too exhausted to yell at Harold? That's your favorite hobby."

"Yelling at Harold isn't a hobby," Carol explained. "It's my duty. The boy needs to toughen up. I saw him carrying a spider outside yesterday; you would have thought it was a baby the way he was fussing over it....I had no choice but to squash the thing...."

NOVEMBER 1, 3:30 P.M. HALL. THE ORDER OF MERIUM

After an hour, the girls finally fell back to sleep, allowing for Jonathan, Shelley, and Carl to crawl out of the sleeping quarters and into the hallway.

"We made it," Jonathan muttered as he collapsed on the floor of the corridor next to Shelley.

But his head had only just touched down on the threadbare carpet when Shelley muttered, "Harold!"

Frantically dusting the walls as he walked, the pudgy boy was fast approaching.

"There's nowhere to hide," Jonathan said as he looked around at the unusually barren section of the hall.

"I'm on it," Carl said as he dove on top of Jonathan and Shelley, covering them and blending into the carpet.

Ouchhhhhhh!!!! Jonathan thought as Carl's elbow smashed into his face. His eyes watered and his teeth clenched from the searing pain, but he didn't make a sound. For always buzzing just beneath the surface was the cold, hard truth—his parents' lives were hanging in the balance.

"Harold is one lousy housekeeper," Shelley mumbled once the boy had disappeared down the corridor. "The hallway's actually dustier than before!"

Covering his left eye with his hand, Jonathan took a deep breath and reminded himself that the pain would soon stop.

Carl squatted next to Jonathan and smiled. "What happened?"

"You elbowed me!"

"I did?"

"Somehow you always seem to injure me," Jonathan grumbled as a vague idea took shape in his mind.

How was it that Carl always managed to hurt Jonathan? Was he just a clumsy kid? Or could there be something more to it, something deliberate even? *Don't be ridiculous*, Jonathan told himself. *What do you know about sizing people up? Nothing, absolutely nothing.* Jonathan pictured himself seated at the back of a classroom in a plain white T-shirt and khaki slacks. He was a boring, middle-of-the-road kid. The beige minivan of humans. Jonathan sighed a long and hearty sigh when a picture of the vice president of the United States flashed through his mind. Jonathan had helped save this man. That's right! He wasn't a beige minivan, not anymore. He was a red sports car, and red sports cars trusted their instincts.

Jonathan watched Carl closely. "How long did you say you've known Hammett again?"

"I didn't say."

"Then why don't you tell me," Jonathan responded.

"A couple of weeks."

"Johno," Shelley interrupted. "What's going on?"

But Jonathan didn't answer, his eyes still trained on Carl.

"Johno, tell me, I'm your partner!"

"Carl's a plant…sent to derail me and this mission."

"Every time my teacher says my name, there's a question mark after it, like she's not quite sure who I am."

—Lisa Takeguma, 13, Toronto, Canada

CHAPTER 10

<098762-PM-LOUC-101>

NOVEMBER 1, 3:49 P.M. HALL. THE ORDER
OF MERIUM

"A plant?" Carl repeated. "Like a fern? Or a cactus?"

"No!" Jonathan answered. "An agent sent to sabotage me...maybe even take me down?"

"I'm definitely not trying to take you down, although I have taken someone down before."

"What?!" Shelley reacted.

Carl nodded. "It was awful, just awful."

"What happened?"

"I accidentally locked my little brother outside during a snowstorm."

"And he froze to death?" Shelley asked before covering her mouth.

"My brother? No, but his imaginary friend Elvis did....He's never forgiven me...even after all these years."

"Your brother had an imaginary friend named Elvis who froze to death in a storm?" Shelley repeated.

Carl nodded. "We wanted to have a funeral for Elvis, bury him in the yard next to Spot, our Dalmatian, but as so often happens with imaginary friends, we couldn't find the body."

Jonathan stared intently at Carl. Was this a performance? Was acting like a clumsy weirdo his cover?

"You're strange," Shelley said to Carl. "Really strange. I'm actually kind of jealous."

"How do you know it's not an act?" Jonathan whispered in Shelley's ear, all the while keeping his eyes trained on the spotted boy.

"Would you excuse us for a second, Charl?" Shelley said as she pulled Jonathan a few feet away. "Johno, as you know, paranoia is my middle name, except that it's not on my birth certificate, nor has anyone ever called me Shelley Paranoia....My point is, I understand why you're worried...because I spend a lot of time worrying about things that aren't actually happening...like aliens landing on Earth and befriending everyone but me...."

"I'm serious, Shells. What do we know about this kid?"

"I know he's not a plant."

"How can you know that for sure?" Jonathan pressed Shelley.

"If there's one thing I can do, it's recognize a fellow underachiever."

"Maybe he's a great actor."

"No, Johno," Shelley stated firmly. "Carl's not a plant, he's just a really bad spy, even by our standards. If he were a plant, he would have taken us out by now."

"I guess that's true," Jonathan acquiesced. "There's just so much on the line....We can't fail... not this time."

"You see these?" Shelley said, pointing to her shoulders. "Let me help you. Let me be your emotional backpack...a stylish one, a *designer* emotional backpack...."

"Thanks, Shells," Jonathan said before looking around. "We need to find a hiding place, somewhere with a good view of the garden."

"Why the garden?" Shelley asked.

"Have you even looked in your copy of *How to Make Great Popcorn in the Microwave*?"

"Of course I have," Shelley answered. "Only I've forgotten every single thing I read, so if you could give me the CliffsNotes, I'd really appreciate it."

"Come on, Shells," Johno said before releasing a long and audible sigh.

"Don't you dare sigh at me, Johno! I deserve better than that! I'm your friend! I'm the life of the party...the party I wasn't even invited to because very few people remember that I exist...even though they should, because I spend a huge amount of time putting my life on the line to keep their country safe, when I could just as easily be at home watching videos about how to hypnotize people with nothing but a spoon, a deck of cards, and a Taser.... What was my point again?"

"I have no idea," Jonathan responded before returning to his plan. "The book says there's a bonfire every day at sundown in the garden. The girls will be there."

Shelley snapped her fingers. "The tower things on the corners! We can watch from there!"

"The turrets," Jonathan said. "Shells, that's actually a good idea!"

"Don't sound so surprised. I have a lot of good ideas; they're just buried beneath terrible ones, so you have to be patient...but as the saying goes, *The patient who's patient gets to live....*"

Jonathan shook his head. "That's not a saying."

"I just made it up."

"I can tell."

"Thank you," Shelley offered with a smile. "This is the kind of moment that makes me happy to be me!"

"I'd be happy to be you too, Shelley," Carl jumped in.

"Don't get creepy, Charl. You know I hate creepy...unless you're a cat. Cats are allowed to be creepy....It's in the Constitution."

"No, it isn't."

"As if Khaki's ever read the Constitution."

"I've never read the Constitution, but I can assure you that our Founding Fathers did not put in anything about cats."

"Clearly a dog guy," Shelley muttered under her breath. "Me? I'm more of a Dr. Dolittle.... All animals love me ... especially ones who don't rely on me to eat ... because I sometimes forget to feed them ... but in a loving way.... Did I mention I'm a part-time vegetarian?"

"Maybe you'd be better off with invisible pets," Carl suggested. "That's what we have at home. I get a new one every year for my birthday."

Shelley smiled. "What a genius way to get out of spending money. Invisible gifts!"

"I hate to interrupt," Jonathan huffed, "but I feel like now might be a good time to remind you both that my parents are sitting in a cell at the CIA."

"That's right," Carl replied, nodding. "I couldn't remember why we were here, but I was afraid to ask because sometimes you look really mean."

"Did I mention that the evidence is stacked against them? That their future looks pretty bleak?"

"No, you didn't," Shelley answered before shaking her head. *Darn those rhetorical questions; they get me every time!*

"My parents are probably going to spend the rest of their lives locked up. Do you know what that means? Every second of every day, I will know that as I walk free, they are behind bars for a crime they didn't even know they were committing."

Shelley grabbed Jonathan's hand. "We won't let that happen."

"Maybe Carl's right," Jonathan supposed. "Maybe unexceptionals have really bad plans? Maybe we shouldn't be trusted?"

"Really, Johno? You're choosing *now* to start listening to Charl?!"

"The *h* is silent, remember?"

"Yes, Charl, I remember!"

"I'm scared we can't do this, Shells....I'm really scared this time...." Jonathan admitted, tears pricking at the corners of his eyes.

"I'm scared, too," Shelley admitted.

"You are?" Jonathan replied.

"But not of failing this mission. I'm scared of being the old Shelley again. The Shelley whose only excitement came from daydreaming. The Shelley whose greatest claim to fame was keeping a goldfish alive...which *actually* is impressive....I can't tell you how many I had to flush before Zelda...and by *flush*, I mean bury in the backyard....Pets deserve burials, even small pets that fit down the toilet. Maybe I should start a campaign to bring dignity back to the goldfish....*DIG A HOLE, DON'T FLUSH.* *Full disclosure: If you have dogs, they will most likely dig up the corpses, eat them, regurgitate them, then eat them again....*"

"Weren't you trying to make him feel better?" Carl interrupted.

"That's what I just did," Shelley answered, her glasses hanging from the tip of her nose. "It's called comforting a friend."

"You can call it that, but that's definitely not what it is."

"Don't mess with me, Charl," Shelley said as she grabbed hold of his shirt. "I don't know karate, or any kind of martial art, for that matter...although sometimes when I'm alone I whisper the word *tae kwon do* for reasons I can't quite explain...but trust me when I say I'll take down anyone who tries to come between me and my bestie...and by *bestie*, I mean best friend...not the best spy...because we're equals...or maybe I'm a little better, not that I tell Johno that since we're best friends and all."

"I wish you'd let go of my shirt. I'd really like to disappear right about now."

Jonathan closed his eyes and whispered, "Me too, Carl. Me too."

"Last week I was mistaken for a garbage can, this week a lamppost....Things are really starting to look up."

—Kate Zan, 11, Ghent, New York

CHAPTER 11

<098762-PM-LOUC-101>

NOVEMBER 1, 7:45 P.M. TURRET. THE ORDER OF MERIUM

An orange glow emanated from the garden. Flames leaped from the bonfire, sparks dancing away into the night. The black sky, peppered with faint stars, loomed. A strong breeze swept through the garden, spreading the thick scent of the flowering trees. There was a tranquility to the moment and for one brief second Jonathan and Shelley forgot where they were and delighted in their surroundings.

"I always wanted to go to camp. Sing songs,

make lifelong friends," Shelley said from their perch in the turret overlooking the garden. "*Camp Lakawanna forever!*"

"Camp Lakawanna?" Jonathan repeated.

"That's the name of my imaginary camp. Sylvia and Lucy are my best friends; we've known each other since we were five. We met singing around the bonfire. One day when we're older with lots of money, we're going to get matching pinkie rings."

"I think you spend far too much time with imaginary people," Jonathan said as a sea of voices began chanting below.

"*Occulta potentia in umbra. Occulta potentia in umbra…*"

One by one, figures cloaked in long velvet robes and red masks marched from the house to the garden. Moving slowly, each stride long and smooth, they encircled the fire pit.

"*Occulta potentia in umbra. Occulta potentia in umbra.*"

"What does that mean?" Jonathan wondered aloud.

"Kill all intruders…unless they're short and cute with glasses?" Shelley suggested.

Carl stepped forward, touching both Jonathan and Shelley on the shoulder. "It's Latin for 'In darkness lies power.'"

"Hold the phone...Charl speaks Latin? And to think my mother told me that 'Life is like a box of chocolates; you always know what you're going to get—chocolate.'"

"That's not the saying," Jonathan said, shaking his head. "Never mind! Carl speaks Latin?"

Carl smiled, exposing his bright white teeth.

"Those are some seriously pearly teeth," Shelley remarked. "I'm going to need the name of your dentist at a later date."

"Can you at least try to stay on track, Shells? Carl with the silent *h* speaks Latin!"

"Actually, I don't," Carl responded. "A few teachers have even questioned whether I speak English."

"Then how do you know what they're saying?" Jonathan asked.

"Harold left his Latin notes on the kitchen counter and I saw 'In darkness lies power' scribbled underneath *Occulta potentia in umbra*."

"So you don't speak Latin?" Shelley clarified.

"No."

"Is it just me or are you a little relieved?" Shelley asked Jonathan.

"When an unexceptional turns out to be exceptional, it rocks the boat...the poorly made, almost-sinking boat...that is our lives...." Jonathan trailed off.

"Occulta potentia in umbra. Occulta potentia in umbra."

"Don't they know any other songs?" Shelley huffed. "Who just sings the same line over and over again?"

Though emotionless and monotone, the voices weighed heavily on Jonathan and Shelley.

They sensed that like an iceberg in the sea, a great deal lurked beneath the surface. And it wasn't good. After all, what kind of people dressed in cloaks and masks? And lived secluded behind a wall, cut off from society, the very society they were so determined to control? *They're the people who rule the world*, Hammett had said. And though frightening, it was a difficult concept to grasp. Was it really possible that the fifty or so people in the garden were orchestrating changes in the stock market, Supreme Court judge appointments, scientific research—all to benefit their own interests?

"If anything goes wrong, they're going to roast us...like one of those chickens on a stick you see at the grocery store," Shelley said, peering down at the garden.

Jonathan nodded, unable to speak, terrified that if he did, something cowardly just might escape his lips. *Let's get out of here! My parents will figure something out....They never have before, but there's always a first*, he imagined himself wailing hysterically. And so Jonathan remained silent, impatiently waiting for his cowardice to pass. He would never be able to live with himself if he just up and left. For he was not only a son trying to save his parents but an operative on a mission. That was the Jonathan Murray he had become, the Jonathan Murray he was proud to be.

And so when the crippling fear finally loosened its grasp, Jonathan turned to Shelley and said, "Hand me the binoculars."

Shelley nodded and then turned to Carl. "Hand me the binoculars."

"What binoculars?" Carl responded.

Shelley turned to Jonathan and repeated, "What binoculars?"

"The ones I handed you on the plane and told you to bring!" Jonathan huffed.

Shelley nodded. "Oh, *those binoculars.*"

"Yes, Shells, *those binoculars.* Where are they?"

Shelley tilted her head and mumbled, "Do you want the truth?"

"Why do you ask questions like that? Has anyone ever responded, *No, lie to me*?"

"Actually, they have....Okay, they haven't, but one day, someone is going to say that, so it's actually not a lie, it's a premature truth...." Shelley rambled.

"Shells, where are the binoculars?"

"On the bench...on the plane..." Shelley admitted sheepishly.

"The plan won't work without binoculars; we're too far away to see the wax on the robes," Jonathan said as he dropped his face into his hands.

"Did you have this plan before—is that why you wanted me to bring the binoculars?" Shelley asked, clearly shocked by Jonathan's foresight.

"No, of course not! I just told you to bring them

because that's what spies do in movies. They dress well and they bring binoculars."

"Have you guys thought about renaming yourselves something a bit more accurate, like the League of Children with Really Bad Ideas, or the League of Children Who Will Probably Get You Killed?" Carl suggested.

"Didn't your mother teach you that if you don't have anything nice to say, you should sew your lips shut, and if you don't have a needle and thread, you should use glue, and if you don't have glue, you should use tape, and if you don't have tape, you should use stickers, and if you don't have stickers—"

"He gets the idea; we all do," Jonathan interrupted before once again focusing on the figures marching around the bonfire. "We're going to have to go down there... get close enough to see the wax on the robes."

"You want to go down *there*? With the psychos?" Carl asked.

"I say we tie some sheets together and rappel down. Sort of like when Rapunzel used her hair to help the prince rescue her," Shelley said before pausing. "I bet her hair was really dirty. How could anyone keep *that much hair* clean? It's impossible! Imagine if she got lice? She'd never get rid of them.... She'd be scratching her scalp for eternity."

Jonathan stared at Shelley and shook his head. "We're not using sheets to rappel down the side of the castle; someone will see us."

"Did I ever tell you about the time I joined marching band?" Shelley asked, raising her eyebrows for effect.

"You're in marching band?" Jonathan asked incredulously.

"I tried out, but unfortunately I was rejected due to my inability to play an instrument. But I really wanted to join and you know how I hate to give up on a dream. So one day I just showed up in the outfit and started marching with them. I didn't even have an instrument. No one noticed a thing."

Jonathan grinned. "If there's one thing an unexceptional does well, it's hiding in plain sight."

"People say youth is wasted on the young. Well, I say intelligence is wasted on the smart. Those kids have no idea how lucky they are!"

—Ayala Tassani, 11, Knoxville, Tennessee

CHAPTER 12

`<098762-PM-LOUC-101>`

NOVEMBER 1, 8:25 P.M. ENTRY HALL. THE ORDER OF MERIUM

"Johno?" Shelley said through the red mask, the black velvet cloak covering her from head to toe. "Do I look okay?"

"You look like a creepy psycho, which just so happens to be what we're going for."

"Is this going to work?" Shelley wondered aloud.

"Probably not," Carl answered. "Which is why I'll be hiding in the bushes."

"Thanks for the support, Charl," Shelley droned

sarcastically as Jonathan slowly cracked open the heavy wooden door to the garden.

The cloaked figures marched in near-perfect unison around the fire. Left foot. Right foot. Left foot. Right foot.

"So we just walk up and act like we belong?" Jonathan said hesitantly.

"Come on, Johno! Don't say it like it's a question; it's our plan!"

"You're right. We need to have confidence or it won't work. People believe what we tell them to believe...and we are going to silently tell them, 'We are just like you.'"

"Good luck with that," Carl said as he slipped past them into the garden.

NOVEMBER 1, 9:03 P.M. GARDEN. THE ORDER OF MERIUM

Walking slowly toward the figures, Shelley suddenly felt the urge to urinate. Why didn't anyone teach spies to pee before embarking on a mission? How come we never saw James Bond taking care of life's many boring necessities like grocery shopping, paying taxes, and using the bathroom?

"*Occulta potentia in umbra*," Jonathan and Shelley chanted beneath their deformed red masks as they walked toward the group marching around the fire.

Jonathan, the first to approach, knew that if he paused too long, he would draw attention. And so he quickly pushed into the circle. A few seconds after which, Shelley followed suit. Round and round they went, chanting, "*Occulta potentia in umbra*." And though dizzying, it allowed them time to scan for the wax drippings.

"*Claudicatis!*" a voice called into the night. "*Claudicatis!*"

What does that mean? Shelley thought as the group came to a sudden halt. *Oh no, what now? What if they break into a routine, like one of those choreographed dances she watched on YouTube? Jonathan will never be able to keep up; he can barely tap his toe, let alone follow dance moves on the fly. Speaking of Jonathan, where was he? Why hadn't they thought about this? There was no way to identify each other! They now appeared exactly like all the others! Look for the girl with the wax drippings*, Shelley thought. *Find her and you'll find*

Jonathan. But what if the girl had noticed the wax and picked it off? Or if she changed cloaks? Ugh, Carl was right, unexceptionals come up with the worst plans!

Staring off into space, overwhelmed by the disaster they had already made of their plan, Shelley suddenly focused in on a clump of wax dribbled along the hem of a cloak two people ahead of her.

And so Shelley retracted her negative thoughts and welcomed a surge of confidence. Yes, they were unexceptionals. And yes, their plans left more than a little to be desired, but that was partly why they worked. They were simple. And people tended to overlook simple.

A bell sounded, prompting the cloaked figures to disperse, scattering across the grounds.

Follow the wax, Shelley told herself. *Don't lose the wax*. Moving through the garden, weaving in and out of trees, Shelley quietly trailed the girl. But it wasn't easy. The soggy grass and newly fallen leaves created sounds, sounds that Shelley worried might draw the attention of the girl she knew as Glenda.

Crinkle. Swish. Crunch. Swish. Crinkle.

The sounds suddenly grew louder; the soft crunch

of the leaves and swish of the grass beneath her feet had amplified. Could it be that someone was walking behind Shelley? Was it Jonathan? Or was it another one of the crazies? But before Shelley could even finish her thought, a hot, searing pain flashed through her head, bringing her to her knees.

Kneeling beside Shelley's limp body, the figure dropped the branch and lifted her mask.

"Oh, Shells, I'm so sorry...."

Jonathan had knocked his partner unconscious in a case of mistaken identity. He had momentarily lost sight of Glenda while trailing her in the garden. And then, when a cloaked figure reappeared before him, he simply assumed that it was her. But it had been Shelley, his partner, who now lay unconscious at his feet while Glenda sat on a bench in the distance. He couldn't undo what he had done to Shelley, but at the very least he could capture the right target, even if it was on the second try. In a swift, almost ballet-like leap, Jonathan lunged toward Glenda, slamming a heavy branch against her back, knocking her to the ground.

Guilty. That was the first sensation that swept through him. Maybe Glenda was a nice person deep down? Maybe she had gotten caught up in the Order of Merium by accident? Maybe he could have subdued her in a different manner? Perhaps a more delicate, friendly manner? Just then Glenda swung her right leg, straight as a board, into the back of Jonathan's knees. Like a pin hit with a bowling ball, Jonathan came crashing down. Wet slivers of grass crept into his mouth as he landed face-first. *What happened?* Jonathan thought as Glenda flipped him over and pinned him down. He tried to move, but it was no use. She was strong and, more to the point, he wasn't.

Picking up a nearby stick, Glenda pushed it lightly down on his throat.

"Who are you?"

"Me?" Jonathan said, desperately trying to buy some time so he could formulate a plan, even a bad plan. At that point he just needed something, anything, to cling to.

"Yes, you," Glenda answered, pressing down on the stick, cutting off his air supply.

"Stop, please, stop!"

"I'm going to ask you one more time: Who are you?"

"Jerry..."

If I'm going down, Jonathan thought, *I'm going down strong.*

"Jerry what?"

"Jerry...Berry."

"Jerry Berry?" Glenda repeated.

No one has a rhyming name! That's not a real thing! Come on, do better, Jonathan thought.

"My parents were really into … humiliating their children … hence my rhyming name."

"Do you know what we do to intruders here at the Order of Merium?"

"Nothing good, I'm guessing," Jonathan answered as Glenda once again pushed down on the stick.

"We make them disappear."

Disappear, Jonathan said to himself. *That's just another word for murder.*

"But only after we've found out every last piece of information they know."

Creak. Crinkle. Crunch.

The others were coming. . . .

"Every two or three years I say something smart. And honestly, it shocks me just as much as my parents."

—Devy Schonfeld, 14, Pasadena, California

CHAPTER 13

<098762-EB-LOUC-101>

NOVEMBER 1, 10:06 P.M. GARDEN. THE
ORDER OF MERIUM

Creak. Crinkle. Creak.

"Shelley!" Jonathan hollered hoarsely, the branch
pushing down on his airway.

But Shelley didn't hear him. She was a lump of
flesh on the ground, eerily still except for the nearly
imperceptible rise and fall of her chest. Jonathan
had knocked out his own partner by accident and
now Glenda, his intended target, was squeezing the
last drops of life from him. Shame engulfed him,

seizing every cell in his body. Never before had he felt such disgust and disappointment in himself.

Creak. Crinkle. Creak.

Carmen and Mickey Murray's faces flashed through Jonathan's mind. Not only were they going to languish in prison, they would soon learn that their son was the world's worst spy. This wasn't how it was supposed to turn out! Jonathan and Shelley had once been successful spies. They had saved the vice president of the United States and the population of England! And yet they couldn't save the Murrays. Pinned down, fighting for each breath, Jonathan felt himself drifting away. Hazy. Confused. Physically depleted. The lack of oxygen propelling him further and further from this world.

Creak. Crack. Snap.

"Ahhhh!!!!!" a voice screeched as the sound of a branch breaking brought Jonathan back to the moment.

Thump!

Trapped beneath Glenda's velvet-clad body, Jonathan struggled to breathe. Hot and sweating, he pushed against her limp frame to no avail. "Help!" he screamed, his voice muffled. Then he paused and wondered, *Who am I calling out to if Shelley can't hear me? Not the other members of the Order of Merium! Please wake up, Shelley.* For even if she couldn't save him, she could save herself.

"Ugh," Jonathan groaned as his temples throbbed and his legs writhed in pain. He hadn't eaten anything in almost twelve hours. He felt drained, too drained to fight. He closed his eyes and prepared for the darkness to take him. Where? He didn't know, but surely anywhere was better than here. Here where he'd failed both his parents and his partner.

Air rushed in as Glenda's body flopped to the side. And though frail, Jonathan felt a sense of calm take hold. Shelley must have woken up. She had rescued him. It felt like a fairy tale, the prince coming to wake Sleeping Beauty, only in this case Shelley was the prince.

Focusing on the face peering down at him, Jonathan suddenly recoiled. "Ahhh!"

"Hey, it's me, Carl, with the silent *h*."

"Where's Shelley?"

"She's making her way over here...she's still a little wobbly."

Jonathan grabbed his neck as he sat up. "What happened?"

"You hit Shelley on the head. Then you tried to take down Glenda. But she had you on your back faster than you can say…pretty much anything… and then she was suffocating you with a branch, or at least it looked that way from the tree."

"You were in the tree?" Jonathan asked. "You're what fell on us?"

Carl smiled. "Yeah, it worked out pretty well, if I do say so myself."

"You jumped onto Glenda to save me?"

Carl shook his head. "Not exactly…The branch broke."

"So you were just sitting there watching her suffocate me?"

"Now that you say it like that…it sounds really bad…maybe even criminal."

Jonathan sighed. What was the point of even discussing this with Carl?

"I wanted to help, really I did…but somehow it just didn't happen…and then the branch broke, beating me to it…."

"Johno," Shelley said as she hobbled toward

them. "You got Glenda? Good! You have no idea how hard she hit me."

"About that…" Jonathan began.

"Let's tie her up before she wakes," Shelley suggested. "There's a shed just past these trees. We can use it to interrogate her."

"Shells, I'm sorry…." Jonathan said as he watched her press her hand to the large welt on the back of her head.

"For what?"

Tell her, Jonathan, the boy screamed to himself. But he couldn't. Not now, not with so much still on the line. Shelley needed to have faith in him if they were to stand a chance of making it out alive. "I'm sorry I…I don't have any aspirin."

"You don't look so good, Johno," Shelley said as she stepped closer. "Sort of like an elderly squirrel who's about to lie down and die."

NOVEMBER 1, 11:02 P.M. SHED. THE ORDER OF MERIUM

"Water…water…I need…water," Glenda whispered as she slowly roused to consciousness. Hands and feet tied together with twine, her mask removed,

149

she looked up to find two unfamiliar faces staring back at her.

"I need water," Glenda said again.

"We don't have any.... We're in a garden shed, in case you haven't noticed," Shelley responded, motioning to their surroundings.

"The Order does not take kindly to intruders."

Jonathan cleared his throat, his voice still hoarse. "I think you've made that point clear. But now, I think it's time to clear up another matter. So what do you say we have a little chat?"

"I haven't much of a choice," Glenda responded as she looked down at the twine binding her hands and legs.

Shelley stepped forward, pushed up her glasses, and announced, "The name's Shelley. Shelley Brown… Darn it! I wasn't supposed to use my real name. I'm going to need to retract that statement and start over as Samantha Powers."

"Shelley Brown…" Glenda repeated.

"I retracted that statement! My name is Samantha Powers!"

"Shells, she's going to know who we are soon enough," Jonathan said before turning toward Glenda. "Do I look familiar?"

"Should you?"

"I guess not since I don't really look like either of my parents," Jonathan muttered before leaning in, staring straight into Glenda's eyes. "The point is, you know my parents. Carmen and Mickey Murray?"

"Who?"

"The couple you tricked into stealing classified documents!"

"Oh," Glenda responded with a smile.

"There's no smiling in here!" Shelley snapped. "Hostages don't smile!"

"So that's what this is about…and yet, I'm the only one here? What about Carol?"

"We realized we only needed one of you, so what can I say? You lost the coin toss," Jonathan covered. "Now, about my parents."

"Your parents are absolute dimwits," Glenda told Jonathan. "We asked them to steal the SATs, not the STS!"

"The SATs?" Shelley muttered.

"The Scholastic Aptitude Test. You know, the college entrance exam?" Glenda explained.

"There's an entrance exam?" Shelley said, shaking her head. "What a bummer! I was hoping it was more of an educational buffet…learn as much or as little as you want, wherever you want."

"I love buffets," Carl chimed in as he stepped forward.

"Ahh! What's that!?" Glenda screeched.

"That's Carl with a silent *h*," Jonathan answered.

"Why does he look like that?"

"The same reason you look like you," Shelley replied. "He came out that way."

Jonathan felt the situation slipping away from him, and jumped in. "Do you realize that my parents are facing life in prison, possibly even death, because you tricked them into committing treason?"

"The end justifies the means. The Order of Merium cannot achieve its goals unless its members are in positions of great power. In order to get there, members must go to the right university, and in order to get *in*, a student must be more than great—he or she must be exceptional."

"Ohhh…that word," Carl remarked. "That's gotta hurt, since you're members of the League of Unexceptional Children and all. Although I still think you should change it to something more direct, like the League of Super-Disorganized Spies."

"Carl!!!!!" Jonathan snapped.

"What? Was I not supposed to bring up the League? I told you I'm not good with secrets….It's your own fault. I warned you….Yet another sign you're bad spies."

"If we're lucky enough to make it out of this alive," Shelley said, stepping closer to Carl, "I'd watch your back…and I realize you can't actually watch your back…I just mean…I'm coming for you…not to physically harm you but to egg your house, dig up your plants, maybe even start a picket line across your lawn...."

"And to think I regarded Carmen and Mickey as the most utterly witless people I'd ever met...Little did I know you guys were out there," Glenda remarked smugly.

"Thank you," Shelley said with a smile.

"That wasn't a compliment."

"Or so you think," Shelley said. "I can turn almost anything into a compliment."

"It's true," Jonathan seconded. "Although I don't know that it's a good thing."

"So Carmen and Mickey actually believed that we were from the Alien Intelligence Agency. What utter dolts! Surely the US government can see that."

"Don't call them dolts," Jonathan barked.

"Yeah!" Shelley added, "It might be true, but it's a lousy thing to say!"

"Listen to me, Glenda. You need to right this wrong," Jonathan declared.

"Right this wrong?" Glenda scoffed. "Who talks like that?"

"Cowboys do...and Jonathan...Well, he's not a

cowboy....I'm pretty sure he's never even been on a horse....He seems more like the donkey type, you know?"

Jonathan lowered his voice, leaned toward Shelley's ear, and whispered, "Was there a point to that?"

"Your guess is as good as mine. Words often come out of my mouth without any warning...or purpose...."

Jonathan sighed and turned back to Glenda. "My parents are good people. They don't deserve this; no one does. And now you're going to fix it."

Glenda shook her head. "I don't think so."

Jonathan stepped closer, his face flooded with anger. "I'm not asking you—I'm telling you. You are going to write a letter explaining exactly what you and Carol did, how the two of you tricked my parents into performing an act of treason."

"And if I refuse?"

"Then we'll be forced to act as both judge and jury for your actions and you'll meet the same fate as intruders within the Order of Merium," Jonathan answered.

"You're not going to off me over a letter. You're not the type," Glenda replied confidently.

Jonathan narrowed his eyes. "Are you sure about that?"

"FYI, my partner is a mentally unstable psychopath who has been known to *off* kittens and puppies just to prove a point," Shelley said. "He's totally toothless."

"She means ruthless," Jonathan clarified.

"No, I mean toothless, as in you've lost all your teeth in fights because you're so tough...get it?"

"But I have all my teeth, so that doesn't make any sense."

"Not your actual teeth, your metaphorical teeth."

"Metaphorical teeth? Do you even know what a metaphor is, Shells?"

"Maybe...maybe not...but I know what teeth are...and I know you don't have any...because you're tough...you're mean...you're an animal who shouldn't be messed with!"

"Exactly, I'm ruthless!"

"You might be ruthless....I can't say for sure until I contact my good friend the dictionary, but I do know you're toothless...even though you have all your teeth...."

"Oh, enough! I can't bear to listen to you two

yammer on any longer! Just hand me the pen and paper," Glenda interrupted. "I'll do it. After all, what's the harm? There's no way you're making it out of the Order alive. No intruder ever has, and no intruder ever will...."

NOVEMBER 1, 11:59 P.M. GARDEN. ORDER OF MERIUM

Glenda sat tied to the chair, a piece of cloth covering her mouth.

"We're sorry to leave you tied up," Jonathan mumbled, "but we can't take the chance of anyone finding out we're here before tomorrow, when everyone's asleep and we can escape."

"Plus, you deserve a little punishment for what you've done," Shelley added.

"What if someone finds her before tomorrow morning?" Carl whispered to Shelley.

"Then we're in big trouble...."

Jonathan popped his head out of the shed, the cold night air greeting him. "Come on," he said as he motioned for Carl and Shelley to follow him.

"Don't get mad, but do we have an escape?" Carl muttered hesitantly.

"Yes, Carl, we have an escape plan," Jonathan replied.

"We're going to hide behind those bushes until day-break, when the Order goes to sleep; then we'll build a ladder to climb over the wall," Shelley answered.

"That plan actually sounds okay," Carl answered as he stepped in front of Jonathan, accidentally tripping him in the process.

"Ugh!" Jonathan grunted as his left ankle turned.

"I'm really sorry! It was an accident."

"I know...I know..." Jonathan mumbled, "but just to be safe, maybe you could stay five to ten feet away from me at all times."

"Sort of like a restraining order, only friendly," Shelley clarified.

"My mom thinks I hurt people to remind them that I'm here. But it's not true! It's all an accident. But ever since I burned down Grandpa's house and broke the windshield on his Cadillac, she doesn't believe me."

"We're going to need details about these events before we move any farther," Shelley replied as she motioned for them to follow her behind the shrubs.

"Yeah," Jonathan seconded. "Definitely going to need those details."

Crouching behind bushes with Jonathan and Shelley, Carl smiled. "Honestly, I think this stuff probably happens to people all the time; they just don't talk about it."

"We'll be the judge of that," Shelley said, motioning for the boy to continue.

"I was in Grandpa's kitchen cooking eggs, when a grease fire broke out...so I threw water on it... which apparently makes grease fires worse. Then I opened a window, hoping the wind would put out the fire, but wind has oxygen in it, which fed the fire. At that point, the smoke was pretty thick, so I grabbed the cat and waited outside."

"And the Cadillac?" Shelley asked.

"I threw a brick through the windshield," Carl said matter-of-factly.

Brow furrowed, Shelley asked, "Why would you do that?"

"Grandpa said he bought a super-strong windshield that even a brick couldn't get through...so I decided to test it out."

"Mental note to Shelltastic: Never invite Charl over to your house."

Jonathan nudged Shelley. "He can hear you."

"Mental note to Shelltastic: Stop saying your mental notes out loud."

Waaa. Waaa.

A siren cut through the garden, electrifying Jonathan, Shelley, and Carl.

"What is *that*?" Carl asked as the trio looked up and saw a dome of black mesh close over the Order of Merium.

"There's an elegance to losing,
one that comes with years and
years of practice."

—Gwen Garnett, 12, Vancouver, Canada

CHAPTER 14

<098762-PM-LOUC-101>

NOVEMBER 2, 12:03 A.M. GARDEN. ORDER
OF MERIUM

"They're locking us in," Carl whimpered, staring up
at the metal lattice.

"They must have found Glenda, which means
they know we're here and they're coming for us,"
Jonathan said.

Flashes of the Meriums' red masks dashed through
the night, momentarily paralyzing Jonathan. *No, no,
no, no,* he repeated to himself as he stood perfectly
still, perspiration running down the side of his face.

"Johno? We need to move!" Shelley whispered, her voice strained and desperate.

But Jonathan didn't move. He stood still, repeating the word *no* over and over again in his mind. He simply couldn't accept what had happened. They had failed. They had failed themselves. But more important, they had failed his parents. Without Glenda's letter, Carmen and Mickey would languish away in a cell. And worse yet, they would think their son had abandoned them, turned his back on them when they needed him most. They would accept that he too believed they were traitors.

"Johno!" Shelley repeated, this time her voice shrill bordering on hysterical.

The boy again failed to react.

"Is he dead?" Carl asked.

"Have you ever seen a dead person standing up? I don't think so," Shelley snapped before turning to Jonathan and grabbing his hand, pulling him as she ran toward the castle.

"Wait for me," Carl called out, trailing behind, safely camouflaged by the trees and greenery.

"There's no way out, Shells," Jonathan muttered as he staggered behind her, his ankle now throbbing.

"There's always a way out...or at least that's what we need to believe...because even though I've never conducted a scientific study, my gut tells me that delusional people are more likely to survive a disaster, because they never give up."

"Oh, Shells, I'm going to miss you...when we're both dead."

"Hey, Dougie? Dougie Downer? Can you press pause on your doom-and-gloom agenda, because I have an idea. If we can't go over the wall, maybe we can go *under*."

"That's a great plan...for gophers....Unfortunately, we're not gophers!"

"I'm talking about the tunnels!"

"The tunnels!" Jonathan responded, eyes widening as he remembered the model they saw in the study.

"*Occulta potentia in umbra...*" voices carried through the garden as they ducked into the castle through a side door.

NOVEMBER 2, 12:23 A.M. CASTLE. ORDER OF MERIUM

Alone in the candlelit hallway, surrounded by frayed tapestries and rusted armor, Jonathan, Shelley, and Carl stopped to orient themselves.

"I think the kitchen's that way," Jonathan said, leaning against the wall, the last remnants of his energy fading fast.

"Guys, how would you feel about me sitting this one out?" Carl asked, his freckled face bright and cheery, seemingly unaware of the situation closing in on them.

Shelley threw her hands up in the air and huffed, "You want to desert us *now*? We're in the middle of...everything!"

"Let him stay, Shells," Jonathan replied, turning toward Carl. "Find a phone. There's got to be at least one in this place. Call Hammett and tell him we need backup! We need help!"

"Got it! Don't worry, guys—you can count on me!"

And just like that, the boy stepped back, fading into a wooden cabinet.

"You think he'll be able to do it?" Shelley asked Jonathan.

"Guys, just so you know, I'm still here. Not that it should affect your answer…"

"Good luck, Carl. May all the invisible letters of the alphabet be with you." Jonathan sighed as he grabbed Shelley's hand and started toward the stairs to the tunnels.

NOVEMBER 2, 1:22 A.M. TUNNEL. BULGARIA

Humid, sludge-covered walls surrounded Jonathan and Shelley as they scrambled through the tunnel. Jonathan lagged behind Shelley, his ankle swollen, his mouth parched, and his head foggy. He wasn't well, but he wanted to escape, so he forced himself to keep going. He told himself that he had been through harder times before and he would get through this too. Never mind that it wasn't true; he had told himself what he needed to hear, words that would fuel another step.

"We have to keep going," Shelley said. "It's either that or rely on Charl!"

Jonathan and Shelley both shook their heads and sighed—a long and heavy sigh. The kind reserved for such annoyances as school talent shows, lines at an amusement park, and teachers who give homework on Fridays.

"The *h* is silent, remember?"

Jonathan and Shelley jumped as a boy's voice emerged from the darkness.

"Did I just hear *Ch*arl remind us *yet again* that his name is pronounced 'Carl'?!" Shelley barked.

"Crazy running into you guys like this, right?" Carl said with the casualness one might expect in a supermarket or even the dentist's office, but not an underground tunnel in Bulgaria.

"Why are you here? You told us you were going to get help! Call for reinforcements!" Jonathan growled, his anger palpable.

"Yeah, about that…looks like it's not going to happen…"

"Gee, you think?" Shelley scoffed.

"I tried.... Actually, I didn't try, I just followed you guys. So no one's coming—well, except for the maniacs. They're definitely coming."

"*Occulta potentia in umbra. Occulta potentia in umbra. Occulta potentia in umbra. Occulta potentia in umbra.*"

"Charl, I hate you. I really do."

"You're trying to use reverse psychology on me, aren't you?" Carl said with a sly smile. "Good news: It's working. I love you, Selley."

"It's Shelley!"

"You sure the *h* isn't silent? It's more common than you think. Carl, Fred, Jerry, Alex—"

"None of those names have *h*'s in them," Jonathan pointed out.

"Or maybe the *h*'s are just invisible?"

"*Occulta potentia in umbra. Occulta potentia in umbra...*"

"We don't have time for this!" Jonathan snapped.

Shelley raised her hand to stop the others from talking. "Do you hear that?"

"The sound of impending doom is kind of hard to miss," Jonathan answered.

"And on that note, I think it's time for me to blend into the background," Carl said, before adding, "But if you need me to relay a message or return a library book or something, just let me know."

Shelley balled her hands into fists and growled. "Stop talking and listen!"

Thhhhhh. Thluck. Thhhhh. Thluck.

"Water's trickling down! That means there's a drain nearby, a possible way out!" Shelley explained as she dropped to her knees and frantically felt around the tunnel floor. Fleshy, phlegm-like lumps passed through her fingers as she searched for the cool touch of metal. "I found it, but it's too heavy. I need your help, Charl!"

"But I'm blending into the background to avoid being killed so that I can live...and return your library books.... What about Jonathan?"

"Khaki's almost dead! He can't lift anything! Come on, Charl, do something right for once!" Shelley said.

Almost dead? Jonathan thought. It was true that he couldn't remember a time when he had felt so depleted, so tired, so utterly devoid of hope. He imagined his skin gray and chalky, his eyes dulled, and his lips cracked with spots of blood breaking through. Maybe he *was* about to die.

"Ugh," Shelley grunted as she and Carl attempted to lift the drain.

Jonathan's stomach sank. This was it. This was the moment their unexceptionalness—specifically their lack of physical strength—was going to get them all killed.

"*Occulta potentia in umbra. Occulta potentia in umbra…*"

"Guys, there's no way we're lifting this drain," Carl said nonchalantly as the chanting grew closer. "Which means this is the end of the road for you two, aka time to pick out coffins. Speaking of which, my uncle can get you a good deal. They don't call him the King of Coffins for nothing."

"*Occulta potentia in umbra. Occulta potentia in umbra.*"

"I'm not ready to die! Or maybe, I'm already dead? Is this…Did I fail heaven's entrance exam? I knew I shouldn't have cut the head off my sister's doll!" Shelley rambled hysterically.

Jonathan looked Shelley in the eye and noted

the disappearance of her irrational optimism, that annoying quality that had always left him with a mixture of envy and irritation. She was unraveling right before his eyes. So he mustered every last ounce of energy he had and presented a self-assured, confident facade. "That doll deserved to have her head cut off.... Wait, that didn't come out right."

"It did if you're trying to sound like one of those crazy people who push strangers in front of trains," Carl explained. "Which is one of my fears: death by train. I'm also afraid of death by hot dog cart, death by cat scratch fever, death by crazed maniacs in a tunnel...."

Jonathan shot Carl a look, took a deep breath, and started again. "What I meant to say was, heaven would be lucky to have you, Shells. But unless you're in a rush to get there, we need to start jumping."

"Jumping?" Shelley repeated.

Jonathan nodded. "If we can't lift the grate, maybe we can break through it?"

"Talk about a khaki-coated genius," Shelley said as the two began jumping up and down.

"*Occulta potentia in umbra. Occulta potentia in umbra...*"

"I've never been one for long good-byes," Carl said as he stepped toward Jonathan and Shelley and threw his arms around them. "Keep in touch...if they don't kill you, that is."

Creeeeaaaakkk. Creeeaaakkk.

"No!" Carl screamed as the grate dropped out from beneath them.

"Shhhhh!!!" Jonathan and Shelley responded as they free-fell through the unknown. Swathed in darkness, all they could do was hope that what awaited them was safer than those chasing them.

Thud!

NOVEMBER 2, 3:17 A.M. ORDER OF MERIUM. BULGARIA

What happened? Jonathan thought as he slowly roused to consciousness. *My head hurts. No, wait—everything hurts*, the boy noted as he opened his eyes. So dark was the room, he wondered if he might be blindfolded. Unable to move, his arms and legs tied tightly, he called out for his friend.

"Shells?"

"Johno?" Shelley offered faintly, "I can't move."

"Neither can I," Jonathan answered.

173

"Guys," Carl chimed in, "I'm here too, just in case you want to check on me."

Jonathan and Shelley shook their heads. Carl was beginning to feel like a shadow, always creeping around behind them. But before they could even finish their thoughts, they heard *it*.

"*Occulta potentia in umbra. Occulta potentia in umbra…*"

"No!" Jonathan and Shelley shrieked as the lights switched on.

Their voices grew hoarse, their veins throbbed visibly across their throats, and their limbs trembled. Seated back to back in chairs, Jonathan, Shelley, and Carl took in the figures surrounding them, cloaked in black velvet floor-length robes and red masks. Deformed and drooping, the masks' features appeared melted, much like a crayon left in the afternoon sun.

"White," Carl mumbled as he looked at the stark floor and walls. "It's my kryptonite. I can't blend with white!"

"Gentlemen…and maybe ladies…it's hard to tell with those outfits," Shelley said as her grubby glasses slid down the bridge of her nose. "I know

174

what you're thinking: Let's just kill these kids and call it a day. Maybe sing that terrible song a few more times and go to bed?"

"Shells? What are you doing?" Jonathan whispered.

"Shelltastic doesn't give up without a fight or a speech," Shelley answered before turning her attention back to the masked figures. "But here's the thing: We're as strong as steel. As loyal as a blind dog. And as devilish as a...deviled egg at a cocktail party...one that has gone bad...as in you're going to have food poisoning for at least two days."

A figure carrying a candelabra stepped forward and slowly lowered the ornate silver antique over Shelley, hot wax dribbling across the back of her hand.

"Ahhhh! Stop it! That hurts!"

"So," Jonathan said, too numb to shout or cry or do any of the other things he would have expected, "*this* is the end."

A scratchy voice replied, "No, *this* is only the beginning...."

"When life gives you lemons and someone tells you to make lemonade, take the lemons and throw them at that person. Then smile."

—Carter Morgan, 13, Stowe, Vermont

<098762-PM-LOUC-101>

CLASSIFIED

NOVEMBER 2, 7:45 A.M. TORTURE CHAMBER. ORDER OF MERIUM

Heavy—why are my legs so heavy? Why is my face so cold, almost numb? These were Jonathan's first thoughts upon waking. Before he had even opened his eyes, he knew something was wrong. Very wrong. Lifting his face from the dusty cement floor, Jonathan looked down and noted the thick black wrought iron chains shackling him to the wall. He was in a cell with a barred window in the door. Sleeping next to Jonathan in the small space were Carl and Shelley. *May they enjoy these last moments of freedom*, Jonathan thought as a twinge of jealousy passed through him. How he longed to close his eyes and return to the safety of his dreams. In truth, he longed to be just about anywhere other than where he was. He had come to the Order of Merium to save his parents, but all he'd managed to do was obliterate his future, as well as Shelley's and Carl's. Oh, Carl, Jonathan thought, remembering the naiveté that had inspired the boy to jump out of the Dark Bird. But of course, Carl hadn't known— none of them had—that the Order of Merium was to be the end of them.

Jonathan lifted his leg and the chain clanged. Unable to move more than a few inches in either direction, he imagined breaking the chains like superheroes so often did in comic books. But Jonathan Murray was no superhero and his life was far from a comic book. Even at his strongest, Jonathan was weak. And today, at this exact moment, he was weaker than he had ever been. His body ached from injuries, hunger, exhaustion, and hopelessness. His mind descended into a fog, slowing his thoughts and dulling his reactions. Shoulders hunched and arms crossed, Jonathan stared off into space, his breath audibly rattling through his chest.

"Tea and bread?" a soft voice came from the other side of the bars.

"What?" Jonathan mumbled, unsure of what he had even heard.

"Would you like some tea and bread?"

It was the boy from the kitchen: round, white, and pasty, with hair even frizzier than Jonathan remembered. Eyes trained on the floor, the boy appeared almost frightened of Jonathan. Was it possible that someone could be afraid of Jonathan? Had he changed so much? Was he no longer the human equivalent of a wet noodle?

"Harold, isn't it?" Jonathan said, before licking his cracked lips.

It would only make his lips drier, he knew that, and yet he couldn't resist that fleeting moment of relief that came when he ran his tongue across his chapped lips.

"How do you know my name?" the boy answered, still not looking up as he placed a tray on the floor and pushed it through a space in the bars.

Jonathan watched Harold closely. There was something about him, something that felt familiar. Harold didn't look like anyone Jonathan knew; it wasn't anything to do with his physicality but rather his energy. The feebleness, the insecurity, the sense that he was ill at ease not only in the world but in his own life—all of it reminded Jonathan of himself. The person he had been before the League, the boy who had gone through life thinking, *I'm a nobody, destined for nothing.*

"How do you know my name?" Harold repeated, his hands visibly trembling.

"We heard you talking to yourself in the kitchen

while you were preparing food for the others," Jonathan explained as he moved his legs, chains clanging.

Harold nodded. "So it's true what they say about you. You're spies."

"Yes," Shelley said as she sat up, rubbing the sleep from her eyes. "But we're not good spies...not that we're bad spies...what I mean to say is we're part of a team of spies that are known for not being good at anything except spying."

"We're operatives for the League of Unexceptional Children," Jonathan added. "It's an elite group that uses the United States' most average children as spies. And I know what you're thinking. Why would anyone want a bunch of average kids as spies? Well, it's because no one notices us, and the few that do, they underestimate us."

Harold furrowed his brow and hunched his shoulders, clearly uncomfortable. "Why are you telling me this?"

"Because we know what it's like not to fit in, to live on the sidelines," Jonathan answered.

"I fit in," Harold warbled as he quelled his trembling hands by making them into fists.

"Harry? Can I call you Harry?" Shelley interjected.

"Must you give everyone a nickname?" Jonathan muttered.

"Nicknames are like ketchup.... They make everything better," Shelley explained to Jonathan before turning back toward Harold. "I can't help but notice that you're the only one awake during the day."

"Someone needs to tidy the house and prepare the food," Harold said. "The Meriums count on me."

"It's nice to be needed, isn't it?" Jonathan said.

"Yes, yes. They need me...very much. I cook and clean and cook and clean...."

Shelley tried to move closer, her chains rustling. "Does anyone else cook or clean?"

Harold shook his head. "No."

"Have you ever helped out in the real world, with projects or missions or whatever they call them?" Shelley continued.

"Once, but I wasn't very good at it. I've never been very good at fibbing."

"Fibbing?" Shelley repeated. "Isn't that just another word for lying?"

Jonathan watched Harold closely; statuelike, he remained eerily still.

"Deep down, do you believe that what the Order of Merium is doing is right?" Shelley pressed on.

Harold finally looked up at Jonathan and Shelley. And for one brief second, they thought they had gotten through to him.

"I need to get back to work. There is much to do before the others wake."

And with that, the boy scurried out.

Hours passed. Jonathan and Shelley talked, then fell silent, then slept, then screamed, then talked again. Tucked away in the basement without any natural light or fresh air, they waited. For what? Nothing good, that was all they knew for sure.

"We're going to die in here," Shelley muttered. "Years from now, some anthropologist is going to find our bones."

"You never know, Shells; we just might get lucky and someone will find us sooner...then at least we'll get funerals."

"Who cares about funerals? That's just one more party I don't get to go to."

"Shells? Have you noticed anything strange?"

"Other than the fact that we're chained to a wall?"

"Carl hasn't said anything in a really long time.... I actually forgot he was here."

"I'm here," Carl mumbled. "But I'm not okay.... I want to go home."

"Charl, I wish I had words to comfort you... and myself... but I don't...."

"Guys, we can't give up hope," Jonathan insisted. "Once you give up hope, it's over!"

"When did you become Mr. Optimism?" Shelley huffed. "Because I don't know if you've noticed, but we're chained to a wall in a dungeon, in the Order of Merium, somewhere in Bulgaria!"

"I always thought it'd be a lawn mower," Carl warbled as his eyes filled with tears.

"I don't understand," Jonathan responded.

"I always thought it'd all end with a lawn mower. That I'd be taken down by some overexcited gardener who didn't see me."

The sound of shoes knocking against old floorboards grew louder and louder until Harold once again appeared, a tray of food in hand.

"I've brought some pancakes in case you're hungry," Harold said quietly as he pushed the food under the bars.

"Did you bring syrup?" Carl asked.

"I'm afraid I forgot the syrup," Harold offered faintly.

"Not to worry, Harry," Shelley replied. "Personally, I don't even like syrup. It's so messy. And when you get right down to it, what is syrup? Tree blood…and I don't know about you, but I don't want tree blood on my pancakes."

"Please stop saying *tree blood*," Jonathan whispered.

"Harry, here's what we want to know. Are you happy?"

"To be honest, I don't really care if you're happy," Carl said in between bites of pancakes. "I just want to go home."

"What do you mean by *happy*? I'm well fed and I'm alive. Isn't that enough?" Harold responded.

Shelley shook her head. "That is so sad, it's almost tragic!"

"Don't you want to do more than just cook and clean?" Jonathan asked. "Don't you want to live life? To see the world outside?"

Harold nodded. "A little...but they won't let me...."

"What if we could help you? What if we took you with us?" Jonathan pressed on.

"Him?" Carl interjected. "Why would we take him with us?"

"Charl, if you don't stop talking, we're going to leave you here!"

"The *h* is silent, remember?"

"*The* h *is silent, remember?*" Shelley mimicked Carl.

"Guys, you're not exactly giving Harold the best impression. We're trying to get him to come with us, so we probably shouldn't lead him to believe we're mentally unstable lunatics who argue with each other."

Red and sweaty, Harold stumbled to find his words, "Um...um...I guess...I mean, I know it's wrong what they do here...but I never thought I would be able to leave, and if I did, who would believe me? Unless of course, I was able to bring the black book."

"Is that like a little black book? Filled with ex-boyfriends and -girlfriends?"

"Shells?" Jonathan interrupted.

"Probably not, but I thought I might as well ask."

"It's the story of everything we've done, sort of like a diary, starting with the assassination of President Abraham Lincoln."

Shelley's eyes bulged. "You guys are responsible for Lincoln's death?!"

Harold nodded.

"Will you help us escape?" Jonathan asked Harold. "We promise to take you with us."

"Yes. But we'll need to move fast. The others will wake soon."

"Then maybe we should wait and try to escape tomorrow when we have more time?" Jonathan asked.

"Tomorrow? You don't have tomorrow," Harold replied.

"What does that mean?" Carl asked.

"By tomorrow they will have made you disappear...forever."

"Never underestimate the power
of the underestimated."

—Jonathan Murray, 12, Evanston, Virginia

CHAPTER 16

<098762-JM-LOUC-101>

"Harold! Where are you going? The sun's setting. We need to get to the garden and pull the lever!" Jonathan said as the frizzy-haired boy started up the spiral staircase.

"The black book. I'm not leaving here without it! The world must know the truth, not just about what we did to your parents, but what we did in the past! We've been an invisible hand, changing the course of history."

"Get the book, just hurry!" Shelley said.

"Hurry? The book weighs twenty-eight pounds!"

"What? Don't you guys have an electronic version? Something we could e-mail ourselves?" Shelley asked.

"No."

"We need the book," Jonathan said. "It's the only surefire way to prove what's happened behind these walls."

"Agreed," Shelley said, turning toward Harold. "We'll meet you by the lever."

NOVEMBER 2, 5:48 P.M. GARDEN. ORDER OF MERIUM

Carl, Jonathan, and Shelley stood anxiously next to the lever, waiting for Harold to arrive. Through the mesh dome, locking them in, they could see swathes of orange, yellow, and red filling the sky as the sun set. And though normally such a sight might relax them, even please them, tonight it terrified them. For once the sun had gone from the sky, the Order would awake and their fates would be sealed.

"Where is he? What's taking so long?" Shelley asked.

"I don't know...." Jonathan mumbled, his heart pounding with adrenaline.

Though physically and mentally depleted, Jonathan was now buzzing from fear and anticipation. What would happen? Could they make it out in time? Would the plan work?

"Shells...if anything happens...and I don't make it out..."

"Johno! Do *not* talk like that! We've come this far, we're going to pull this off...and even if we don't, I'd rather go down hoping, believing that somehow, someway things will be okay...so don't take that away from me...please."

Jonathan nodded, unable to put into words what he wanted to say. It was something along the lines of *Thank you, you're my best friend, and there's no one I'd rather "disappear" with than you.*

"He's here! Harold's here!" Shelley squealed as she spotted the sweat-drenched boy, lugging what looked like a medium-sized black box but was actually a leather-bound book containing the crimes of the Order of Merium.

"Now, I know everyone gets pretty peeved when I

use the *p*-word, but how exactly are we *planning* on getting over the wall?" Carl asked.

"Charl! You were with us when we came up with the plan!" Shelley snapped.

"Yeah, but I don't listen that much when you guys talk.... Your ideas kind of scare me."

"We must pull the lever! The sun is almost gone!" Harold whimpered. "And once it's gone..."

"Do it," Jonathan instructed Harold.

And so Harold placed his callused white hand on

the lever and pulled. Immediately the sound of metal grating filled the air. It was loud, too loud to ignore. Harold then took the large black book and swung with all his might against the lever.

"What are you doing?" Jonathan asked, his upper lip covered in perspiration.

"We must disable the lever if we're to stand a chance of getting out of here," Harold replied as he once again banged the heavy black book against the bar, leaving it dangling from the wall.

Shelley turned to Carl. "Help Harold get the book over to the wall. We'll meet you there as soon as we can."

Running through the garden, toward the shed where they had interrogated Glenda, Jonathan felt his chest tighten. The sound of the metal dome retracting was so loud. And the sun, the sun was almost gone. The Order was awake. He could feel it in his bones.

NOVEMBER 2, 6:01 P.M. GARDEN SHED. ORDER OF MERIUM

Shelley pushed the wheelbarrow as Jonathan loaded old crates, planting pots, and rope onto it.

"I'm worried...." Shelley muttered. "I don't

want to disappear....I feel like I've only just arrived in this world."

Jonathan longed to hug Shelley and tell her that he too thought they were doomed. But he remembered what she had said: No matter what happened, she didn't want to lose hope.

"Never underestimate the power of the underestimated," Jonathan said with a smile as they pushed the wheelbarrow out of the shed and into the garden.

Shrieks similar to those Jonathan and Shelley had heard from a hyena on a nature program filled the yard. Long gone were the monotone chants of *"Occulta potentia in umbra."* The Order was now at war, and as such, released sounds that one might describe as hair-raising, as in they actually raised the hair on the back of Jonathan's and Shelley's necks.

Through the trees and shadows of the night came flashes of red.

"Hurry, Johno!" Shelley pleaded as Jonathan and Carl stacked a bag of fertilizer atop the wheelbarrow, then an old wooden crate, and finally a terra-cotta planter. It was wobbly and unsafe, but it was their only shot.

"You ready, Shells?"

"I was born ready.... Well, not for this... but for other things, like being rich and famous...." Shelley trailed off as she wrapped old rope around her arm and then slowly started up the makeshift structure.

"They're getting closer.... Hurry, dear girl, hurry," Harold pleaded as Shelley mounted the bag of fertilizer, then the crate, and finally the terra-cotta pot. Standing uneasily at the top, she placed her hands on the mossy green wall, her fingers just shy of the top. Palms sweating, heart pounding, Shelley lifted her heels until she was standing on her tiptoes.

"I can't reach," Shelley whimpered as the shrieks of the Meriums echoed through the night.

"Just a little higher, Shells; you've just about got it."

"They're almost here!!" Harold said.

You can do this, Shelley Brown, she told herself. *You're an unexceptional, which is to say, you're actually kind of special. You come through where others fail. You may not be smart or popular or athletic, but somehow, someway, you always manage to pull off the impossible.*

"I got it," Shelley said as she slowly pulled herself up to the top of the wall. Looking out over the garden, she saw the Order swarming like locusts, desperate to find them.

"Drop the rope," Jonathan called out.

Shelley dropped the rope, waited for Jonathan to grab one end, and then, holding the other end, she rappelled down the wall.

Once down, she secured the rope to a tree and waited. Next over was Carl, then Harold. And though she felt relief to see them, she also felt panic—terror, actually. Would Jonathan make it in time? She needed him. His family needed him. The world needed him—whether they knew it or not.

"Johno! Hurry! Please hurry!" Shelley cried.

"I'm trying," Jonathan called out as he saw a masked figure running toward him. Jonathan was empty, both physically and mentally, and he had a twenty-eight-pound book strapped to his back. Why hadn't he made Carl or Harold carry it? he thought. Bad planning, that's why! Why couldn't he have a good plan just this once, one that was easy, one that went smoothly. But of course, life wasn't smooth, and espionage was *definitely* never smooth.

Pulling himself up the wall using the rope, Jonathan watched the masked figure get closer and closer. He wasn't high enough up the wall; the figure could still reach him.

"*Occulta potentia in umbra,*" the figure chanted, grabbing hold of Jonathan's foot.

"No!!!!" Jonathan screamed as he felt himself slipping down the rope.

Harder and harder the figure pulled while Jonathan fruitlessly tried to escape. *This is it*, Jonathan thought, *you're not going to make it.*

"Johno!!!!" Shelley's voice carried over the wall.

The figure turned and looked up, momentarily distracted by Shelley, giving Jonathan a sliver of a window to pull back his foot and kick the figure in the face. As the masked person dropped to the ground, Jonathan's adrenaline surged, fueling him up the rope to the top of the wall. But once at the top, Jonathan realized he wouldn't be able to rappel down using the rope, for there was no longer any weight on the inside wall to hold him.

"How am I going to get down?" Jonathan called to Shelley, Harold, and Carl below.

"Throw the book first, then jump—we'll catch you," Harold offered.

And so Jonathan threw the twenty-eight-pound

book to the ground and then closed his eyes and jumped. He had imagined the three of them catching him softly with their arms.

"Ahhh!" Shelley screamed as Jonathan landed atop her, spraining her ankle and breaking her wrist.

It wasn't a perfect landing. It was actually a rather imperfect landing. But it worked, and in the end, that's all that mattered.

NOVEMBER 4, 9:03 A.M. THE WHITE HOUSE. WASHINGTON, DC

"Can you believe this is actually happening?" Shelley asked Jonathan as they waited inside the White House, President Arons outside in the Rose Garden with Harold, the black book, and pretty much every reporter in the country.

"I'm just happy my parents are back home," Jonathan responded.

The Murrays had been released following the verification of Glenda's letter and the black book. Not that Carmen and Mickey had any idea who had orchestrated the whole thing. Jonathan thought it better they find out along with the rest of the world.

(Full disclosure: The Murrays considered being on television the ultimate sign of success.)

Shelley smiled. "We're about to be famous… super-famous.… From now on, people are going to remember us.… They might even call us by our correct names."

"No more Jerry and Sally or Sue and Jeffrey," Jonathan added.

"Yeah," Shelley agreed.

"But also, no more League…" Jonathan muttered.

"What do you mean?" Shelley replied.

"It's kind of hard to be a spy when you're famous."

Shelley paused. She hadn't thought of that. She had just assumed that they would keep working for Hammett and the League of Unexceptional Children. Everything would be the same, only the world would know that they were special. They were somebodies.

"I've spent my whole life with this feeling that I'm not who I'm supposed to be, that the life I wanted was impossible…so I made up stories, I told lies…anything just to escape that feeling for a second.…"

Jonathan nodded.

"Because the feeling's so heavy, it's like a weight, always there to bring me back to reality . . . and reality's never been much fun. But then again, it's hard to have fun when your only friend can't speak or even breathe air."

Jonathan tilted his head. "I don't follow."

"Zelda the goldfish."

"Well, at least you had Zelda. That's one more friend than I ever had."

Shelley started tearing up.

"Shells, please don't cry, because then I'll cry, and then we'll be known as the crying spies . . . and that's not the kind of international nickname I want for us."

Shelley's tears came faster and heavier.

"What is it? I've never seen you like this before," Jonathan said as he dabbed Shelley's cheeks with a tissue.

"I'm crying for the girl I used to be . . . the girl who thought she was a nobody."

"But not anymore, Shells! In a couple of minutes the whole world is going to know who we are! Our parents! Our classmates! Strangers! Everyone!"

"Yeah!" Shelley said excitedly. "Maybe they'll

build a statue in our honor! And everyone will have to bow when they pass by!"

"I'm not so sure about that....It feels a little dictator-ish," Jonathan replied.

Shelley shrugged. "You might be right."

"We don't need a statue. Our names are going down in history!"

"But we'll lose this...we'll lose the League," Shelley added.

"Yes," Jonathan said. "But you'll get what you've always wanted. You'll be recognized for who you are."

"What about you? Isn't that what you want too?"

"I used to think so, but it turns out all I really wanted was a friend." Jonathan smiled shyly. "And now I have one."

Shelley pointed to the door to the Rose Garden. "So you're doing this for me?"

"That's what friends do. They help each other realize their dreams."

"What if it's not my dream anymore? What if I'm happy just being Shelley Brown, international lady of espionage?"

Jonathan smiled. "But no one will know that.

To the outside world, you'll still be boring old Shelley Brown."

"Yeah," Shelley mumbled, peering over her glasses at Jonathan. "But when it comes to Shelley Brown, whose opinion could possibly matter more than Shelley Brown's? And I know that I'm awesome."

"I couldn't agree more," Jonathan said. "But are you sure you want walk away from all that? I know how much you want to be famous."

"As the saying goes, fame can't buy you happiness, but money can buy you groceries, which you can use to feed your best friend after a long day of spying and really, what's better than that?"

"Nothing," Jonathan agreed as the two turned away from the door to the Rose Garden, leaving the president, reporters, and international acclaim behind.

"Come on," Shelley said as she looped her arm through Jonathan's, "let's get back to headquarters...."